About Riya Lakhani

Riya Lakhani is the pen-name of a husband-and-wife writing team who both work in television—which was the backdrop for their own romance. They work in TV news—one as a presenter, the other as a producer. In the best courtship tradition, on their first date they were accompanied by a chaperone! They live in the heart of the UK with their two children, and draw upon their own background of mixed cultures for their inspiration. They say writing romance is the perfect antidote to the doom and gloom of TV news because there's always a happy-ever-after.

'So you're the missing reporter who should have been here forty-five minutes ago, are you?'

Rani gave him an embarrassed, shy smile. She felt weak, vulnerable, and very stupid for smiling like a silly schoolgirl.

'You'd better get in, then,' he said, and opened his door. 'Come on. If you want that interview you'd better hurry—we're running late!'

Rani lowered her head and slipped cautiously into the back seat.

'I'm very sorry I'm so late. I got delayed watching one of your movies!' It was half true, she thought, and it sounded better than admitting to oversleeping on the sofa.

'Interesting. Which one?'

'*Sacred Heart.* It's my favourite.'

'Mine, too,' replied Omar, looking straight at her.

Rani could sense his gaze upon her. She'd waited ten years to be this close to him, and if the feelings growing in her body were anything to go by it was worth the wait…

A Date with a Bollywood Star

Riya Lakhani

All the characters in this book have no existence outside the imagination of the author, and have no relation whatsoever to anyone bearing the same name or names. They are not even distantly inspired by any individual known or unknown to the author, and all the incidents are pure invention.

First published in Great Britain 2013
by Mills & Boon, an imprint of Harlequin (UK) Limited.
Harlequin (UK) Limited, Eton House, 18-24 Paradise Road,
Richmond, Surrey TW9 1SR

ISBN: 978 0 263 23459 6

Harl ... ble
and ... able
fore...
lega...

Prin...
by C...

This is Riya Lakhani's fabulous first book for Mills & Boon® Riva™!

Thank you to everyone who made it possible.
You know who you are, and we know where you live!

Thank you to everyone who made it possible.
You know who you are, and we know where you live!

CHAPTER ONE

RANI LET HERSELF into her apartment, switched on the lights and then closed all the blinds in the open-plan living room. Being on the eighth floor gave some privacy but you never knew who might be looking. It was a neat and tidy flat that she was happy to call home. Everything was just where she wanted it: knickers in the knickers drawer, shoes on their racks, suits pressed and bagged hanging in colour order in the wardrobe. It was exactly the way she liked it. Although perhaps it might be nice to find a little disarray with the bedclothes now and again, she thought naughtily to herself. She fitted the flat and it fitted in with her busy life in the centre of London. Yes, she had everything she wanted: the career in journalism, a best friend she could call on at any time of the day or night and a mother who phoned religiously every Sunday morning at eleven on the dot.

The red light on the answer phone was flashing. Rani walked towards it, sat down on the sofa, took off her overly high heels, which made her smile just to hold them, and hit the play button. It was her office.

'Rani, it's Tony, we've an urgent job for you. Omar Khan is back in town and we didn't know. He's making a movie and we've got just ten minutes with him tomorrow morning at eight-thirty. He's staying at Claridge's.

Don't be late. If I don't hear from you then I'll assume you'll be there. Bye.'

Rani replayed the message. She had definitely heard correctly. Omar Khan—she had to interview *the* Omar Khan. He didn't normally give interviews. She thought about the rumpled bedclothes again. Omar Khan had been her idol when she was growing up. He had been the leading man in Indian films for years. She remembered the first movie of his she'd seen, *Sacred Heart*. It was still her favourite of all time and now she was actually going to meet him. She dived off the sofa towards the DVD shelf. She realised her hands were shaking as she traced along the titles looking for the film. Got it! She turned on the plasma, put the DVD in and hit the play button. As the soundtrack started she walked to the bathroom and began taking off her make-up and washing her face.

What an evening she'd had! Press passes to the hottest club in London where she'd danced herself silly and now she was going to meet the heart-throb from her teens. The haunting music wafted around her head and she closed her eyes imagining the images playing on the screen. The leaves falling, two horses being ridden through the wood; on one was Keshina Chandrapour, the leading female Bollywood star at that time. On the other, Omar Khan. She could see his chestnut horse in her mind, the slow-motion shots of hooves hitting the ground, throwing up leaves, and the bright sunlight dancing through the trees. The overflowing sink brought her back to the bathroom.

'Oh, stupid!' she said to herself and threw a towel onto the floor to mop up the water. Rani put her dressing gown on and walked back into the living room with a blanket from her bed and curled up on the sofa. Research, she told herself as she settled down to watch the rest of the movie.

The phone rang and Rani ignored it. She rolled over and back into the dream she had been enjoying. Riding through the wood on the back of a horse, her arms clasped around the waist of the man in front of her. As the horse thundered along she was holding him tight for fear of falling off, and just because she could! She tried to regain the sensation she'd had of her head against his hot muscular back but the phone kept ringing and breaking the concentration of her sleepy mind.

'Oh, what now?' She sighed as she finally opened her eyes. Rani suddenly realised that she'd fallen asleep on the sofa. Her thoughts flashed from one thing to another: the fun of her night out, the late-night answer-phone message, the aches in her body from sleeping crunched up, the very vivid dream, the message on the answer phone! In an instant she was sitting bolt upright and cursing.

'Oh, no, the interview!' she exclaimed as she lunged for the phone. But it stopped ringing before she could reach it. Her eyes immediately searched out the clock in the middle of the bookcase. It was eight-thirty a.m. and she was late.

'No, no, no, this can't be happening,' she moaned, clutching her head. A one-to-one interview with the man whose face she had plastered all around her bedroom wall as a girl and she was late. Not just late but massively, inexcusably late. The phone clicked into answer-phone mode and began recording.

'Rani, I do hope you're not listening to this on loud speaker.' It was her boss, Tony, and she knew why he was calling. 'You should be at the interview NOW!'

Tony knew her too well. 'Khan's PA has phoned and says they have a car waiting to take them to the set and it's leaving in twenty minutes. Don't blow the interview. Oh, and one last thing—make sure you ask him about his dad. We've just heard the old goat is publishing a kiss-and-tell book. That should put the cat among the pigeons!' And the message ended.

She was wide awake now and could feel the tension and stress building inside her body. Breakfast was out of the question, so was having a shower, and, worse still so was changing her clothes. Rani looked down and realised that beneath her dressing gown she was still wearing the red dress from the night before. There really was no time to change. But she could at least brush her teeth and put on fresh knickers!

Three minutes later and slamming the door closed on her flat, Rani ran to the lift and waited. She drummed her fingernails against the doors with impatience. 'Come on, come on,' she said out loud to the lift. There was one stroke of good luck—as she ran out of the apartment block and into the street there were plenty of black cabs and she quickly hailed one.

'Claridge's and please hurry,' she urged the driver.

As the cab did a U-turn and headed off towards the Marylebone Road Rani began applying her make-up. There was an art to putting it on in a moving car and she had perfected it after years of practice.

'Running late?' the driver asked over his shoulder.

'Just a little,' Rani replied, trying not to open her mouth too wide as she put on her lipstick.

'A bloke, is it?'

'Yes,' she said, 'that sort of thing.'

'Don't worry, love, he'll still be there. You're worth waiting for.'

Rani blushed a little and smiled. *I may not have prepared any questions for the interview*, Rani thought to herself, *but at least my make-up is OK*. She looked at her watch and began tapping her fingers on the window. It was five to nine. As the cab moved slowly through the morning traffic Rani's heart raced. She could feel the butterflies in her stomach and the pulse of blood in her temples. She tried to breathe slowly to steady herself.

'Here you go, love, Claridge's. That'll be fifteen quid.'

Rani thrust a twenty-pound note into the driver's hand and opened the door. She was already halfway out of the cab as he called after her.

'What about your change?'

'Keep it,' she replied breathlessly and carried on out of the taxi and up towards the hotel.

Head down like a charging beast, Rani whizzed past the top-hatted doorman and pushed on the hotel's revolving door just as a group of people began pushing the other way. She was spun back out and onto the pavement landing in a very unglamorous heap as her ankle gave way. The contents of her handbag spilled out and she watched in horror as her favourite lipstick rolled off the pavement, into the road, and down a drain. Tears filled her eyes. What else could possibly go wrong?

A hand came down towards her and she instinctively took it and looked up at the same time. She felt a surge of adrenalin course through her body as the powerful arm lifted her to her feet and she looked into the eyes of the handsome man helping her. They were a brilliant green. Still as rich and mesmerising as they had ever seemed on the screen of her local cinema.

'Are you OK?' he asked, with genuine concern in his voice.

'I think so,' Rani replied as she hobbled to her feet and clutched onto the stranger's arm for support. But he was no stranger to her.

'Here, let me help you,' he said, and began to gather the spilt belongings together. He collected her keys and purse and mascara and pieces of her mobile phone.

'I don't think this will be making any calls for a while!' he said, holding up the broken bits in the palm of his hand.

'Thank you. You're very kind, Mr Khan,' Rani said, having regained her composure.

One of his entourage tugged at his sleeve.

'We really must be going. We'll be late,' the flunky said, pulling at the sleeve again.

Omar Khan didn't move. It wasn't unusual for women to recognise him and sometimes fall at his feet. But never in such a dramatic fashion.

'You really know how to make an entrance, don't you, Miss…?' he asked, his sentence rising to a question at the end.

'Rani, Rani de Silver,' she said. Omar felt another tug on his coat as he was being dragged towards his waiting car.

'It was a pleasure meeting you,' he said as he was almost manhandled into the back seat by his PA. 'Peas,' he added as the door closed.

Rani stood outside the hotel. Peas? What did he mean? The tinted electric window slowly lowered to reveal Omar Khan's beaming smile.

'For your ankle. A bag of frozen peas—that should help reduce the swelling.' And with that advice the window started to close. Rani suddenly realised what on earth she was meant to be doing at the hotel. She hobbled towards the car as quickly as she could, wincing at the pain in her ankle, and shouting at it to stop.

'Wait, please stop, I'm here to interview you,' she called, realising as the words left her mouth just how pathetic they must have sounded. The window began to lower again.

'Thank you for the medical advice, Mr Khan,' Rani began, her voice more controlled this time, 'but I'm actually here to interview you. Rani de Silver of the *London Review.*'

'Hold on a moment, George,' he said, tapping the headrest of the seat in front of him. The car had hardly moved any distance but reversed the few yards back to where Rani was standing. Omar Khan lowered the window completely.

'So you're the missing reporter who should have been here forty-five minutes ago, are you?'

Rani gave him an embarrassed, shy smile. She felt weak, vulnerable and very stupid for smiling like a silly schoolgirl.

'You'd better get in, then,' he said and opened his door. 'Come on. If you want that interview, you'd better hurry—we're running late!'

Rani lowered her head and slipped cautiously into the back seat. As Omar introduced the other occupants Rani found herself staring into his eyes.

'My manager,' he said, indicating the woman sitting next to him. 'My PA,' he said, pointing to the woman sitting in the front seat, 'and George, my driver and minder when I'm in London.' The two women looked at Rani but said nothing. They didn't need to. Their blank disapproving faces said it all. Obviously they were not impressed by the latecomer joining them for the ride, dismissing her as another flirt after his attention. Rani knew what they were thinking and felt she needed to apologise.

'I'm very sorry I'm so late. I got delayed watching one of your movies!' It was half true, she thought, and it sounded better than admitting to oversleeping on the sofa.

'Interesting. Which one?'

'*Sacred Heart.* It's my favourite.'

'Mine too,' replied Omar, looking straight at her.

Rani could sense his gaze upon her. She'd waited ten years to be this close to him and if the feelings growing in her body were anything to go by it was worth the wait.

'Why?'

'Because it was my big break. My chance to escape. Now what else do you want to know?' he said, changing the subject. 'How do I feel when I have to film my bedroom scenes? What's it like being voted Steer with the Rear of the Year three times in a row? Did I really do my own stunts in *Bombay Sweethearts*? Who do I think is the better actor—me or Amitabh Bachchan?' He stopped just long enough to take a breath and then proceeded to answer all the questions. 'Nervous, embarrassing, yes and me!' he said. 'Is that the sort of thing you're after?'

'Actually I was wondering why you've never spoken publicly about your life here in England, you know, before you moved to Pakistan and India to became a big Bollywood star?' There was silence. Eyes flitted around the confined space of the car but Rani held her ground. 'Is there something you're hiding?'

'You're good, Miss de Silver, and straight to the point. I like that,' Omar said in a Lancashire accent, dropping any pretence of his subcontinent drawl. It was easy to slip back into his Mancunian dialect. Twenty-four hours in England and he was rolling his shoulders and dropping the façade that the world looked upon. There was a certain relief in being able to be himself with no pretentions. But he wasn't going to let it all go just like that, not in front of a journalist. He'd come from the streets where you had to have a head on your shoulders. He could charm the birds from the trees and he wasn't about to let a posh talking reporter under his skin, no matter how attractive she was. He stopped staring at her. Realising he'd been eyeing her up.

'Thank you,' she said politely in her crispest voice. The money her father had spent on her education wasn't wasted. He was typically Asian like that.

'Get a good education and then you can go anywhere,' he was always telling her when she was growing up.

Chivingham School did exactly as it said in the prospectus: *'We turn girls into young ladies.'*

'Perhaps we should start again. We seem to have got off on the wrong foot,' she said, trying not to show the effect he was having on her.

'Sadly for you, Miss de Silver, you've only the one foot to do anything with at the moment,' he said, pointing at her uninjured leg. He couldn't resist; that was the clown in him, always wanting to be the centre of attention. Always wanting to make people laugh. That was how he'd survived school, when he'd bothered to attend. It certainly wasn't his academic achievements that had got him through.

The others laughed along with him. But as he saw Rani's mortified reaction to his joke he stopped.

'I'm sorry, I shouldn't have said that. You're quite right—let's start over,' he said apologetically, slipping unconsciously back into his Bollywood accent. 'As you can see we are both captives in the car until we reach the film set, so please ask what you like.'

Rani hoped he would be true to his word and, when he was answering the more general questions she knew she had to ask, he was. Gently she edged towards more personal ones trying to uncover something of his private life.

'Tell me about your mother,' she asked. He visibly baulked and gave a dismissive answer.

'People don't want to read about that,' he said, smiling an unconvincing sort of smile. Rani tried again.

'What about your father. He was from Lahore, wasn't he?' His eyes instantly contracted at the mention of his father.

'Yes, he was,' Omar answered coldly without offering anything more.

'I understand he's publishing a book about you.'

The car almost crashed off the road as George heard the words that had been forbidden to be spoken by anyone. The shocked reaction from all of the other people in the car was plain to see but it didn't stop Rani from soldiering on.

'Have I said something I shouldn't have?' she asked innocently, knowing full well she had.

Omar said nothing. George said nothing. The PA said nothing. In the end the manager squeezed a few words from between her thin pursed lips.

'It's not a subject Mr Khan is willing to discuss.'

Clearly he's got issues, Rani said to herself. *This is like pulling teeth, and I thought it would be fun! Who was I kidding? He's just a working class wide boy with the manners to match!* She began to despair that she would ever get beneath the guard he was putting up.

He kept deflecting each of her advances with stock answers as if he were swatting at flies. More in desperation than in hope, she had one last go.

'Have you ever said I love you and not meant it?'

There was silence. Not just the sort of silence you got when there were no sounds, but the sort of silence only possible in a vacuum. Rani felt as if all the air in the car had been sucked out and they were living the very last second of life. She scrunched up her eyes waiting for the response, whatever it would be. And then it came.

'I'm an actor, of course I have.' Rani felt the air rush back into the car and breathed again. *Good answer*, she thought. *Perhaps we're getting somewhere after all.*

'What about you, Miss de Silver?' Omar asked with a tight smile.

Rani was a little taken aback as she wasn't used to having the tables turned on her like this.

'Call me Rani, please,' she said, trying to buy a bit of thinking time. She could feel her face glowing with embarrassment.

'Well, Rani, yes or no?' Omar rephrased the question and pressed his advantage.

Rani squirmed.

'No, but I've heard it,' she replied rather coyly. She felt the blood pumping through her body.

Omar was intrigued but said nothing.

Rani was relieved when the car finally arrived at the film set and she could escape from the claustrophobia she felt. She needed to put some distance between herself and Omar Khan, demigod, movie star and, by all accounts, show-off. Her thoughts and feelings were confused and tangled with her need for professionalism and she required space to unravel the mess. After all, she'd waited years for this moment and now it was here she was unsure of how to proceed. As soon as the car door opened there was a swarm of assistants all queuing up to take orders and do his bidding. Rani couldn't help but see many of them were young, pretty women. It felt quite alarming as she was caught up in the middle of them and washed away like a boat from the shore. As she disappeared from view she did manage to say goodbye.

'Thank you for your time, Mr Khan. Good luck with the filming,' she cried out. After all, whatever she felt about him she'd been brought up to be polite.

'You'd best come this way, miss.' It was George, the driver. He ushered her away, supporting her limping form with an arm the size of a large tree around her waist and leading her towards a long trailer.

'I've never been on a movie set before; I've only ever seen these mobile home things, well, in the movies!' Rani said with surprise. George laughed.

'You get used to it, miss. They're nothing special, not if you end up living in them week after week. Here, let me help you.' And he gently lowered her into a chair and found a stool to prop her swollen leg on.

'Thank you, George, really, I'm fine.'

She looked around her at the trailer. There were photographs of Omar Khan in frames dotted about the place and Rani realised she must have been shown into his trailer. There were pictures of him with various famous people and glamorous women, the heads of state of India, Pakistan, the British prime minister and even one with him playing golf with two former American presidents. But the one that caught her eye was of a little Indian girl standing in front of an old brick building. The picture looked very old and the girl looked as if she was no more than eight. Rani squinted her eyes as she strained to read some lettering carved into the building behind the little girl and could just make out a few of the letters. It looked like *poor*. Rani gently picked up the tatty wooden frame to take a closer look. As she did the door to the trailer opened quickly, which shocked her so much she let go of the picture. She grabbed for it as it fell towards the floor but she couldn't catch it. Rani winced as the glass shattered and the frame broke in two.

'Sorry!' she exclaimed, looking towards the door. It was Omar Khan's manager.

She was a woman in her late forties, smartly dressed but very offhand. She huffed and looked disapprovingly at Rani and the picture.

'Don't be. I don't know why he keeps the scrappy little thing, anyway,' she said. Rani hobbled around trying to find something to collect the broken pieces of glass in. George entered the room from the bedroom at the back of the trailer.

'What's going on?' he asked. The manager looked at Rani and pointed.

'This clumsy girl's smashed Sahib's treasured picture, poking her nose into his things. That's reporters for you,' she said in a gleeful tone.

Rani looked at George for support.

'It really wasn't like that. It caught my eye, that's true, and I was wondering who the photograph was of. Then I was startled and it slipped from my hand. I'll repair it or replace it, of course,' she insisted.

'Come on, I'll give you a hand tidying up and then we'd better get you out of here before you do any more damage,' George said, smiling kindly at Rani. She was pleased to be believed and her relief showed across her face.

'They're about to start the day's filming, miss, so I'll find you somewhere you can sit without getting in the way,' George said.

The manager made a very loud sulky sound so she was sure they had heard her and stormed out of the trailer.

'Watch her, miss, she's a right one. I wouldn't trust her as far as I could throw her, and I don't think that's very far, judging by the size of her!'

Rani began to laugh but felt unsure if she should.

'Oh, don't you worry, she knows how I feel about her, but you'd do well not to let on too much. She's a dragon. Thinks it's her job to stop attractive women like you getting too close to Mr Khan, if you don't mind me saying how attractive you are,' George added. He began to blush.

Rani smiled.

'Not at all, George. That's very kind of you. It's nice to be appreciated and thank you for the warning about her,' Rani said, standing up with the pieces of the frame and the old photograph in her hand. 'Who is it?' she asked.

'It's his mother,' George said. 'Come on, I'll show you to your seat.' And with that he opened the door to the trailer and helped Rani down the few steps.

The set was busy and noisy. From where Rani was sitting it looked like a headless chicken convention. There were people rushing in all directions and saying all sorts of things but not much seemed to be actually happening. Suddenly the noise stopped and the set fell totally silent. Omar walked in, his head bowed, listening to the man walking with him. They both stopped, smiled at each other and then the man walked away, leaving Omar standing alone at the bottom of a wide staircase.

'Lights, camera, action,' the other man bellowed. *He's obviously the director*, thought Rani as she stared at the scene. A pretty girl wearing a sari ran onto the set and rushed past Omar. She was in floods of tears. He held out a hand to grab her by the arm as she tried to climb the stairs, pulling her back towards him. The girl struggled for a moment and then melted into his arms as he pulled her to his chest. Their lips were just about to meet when the director yelled.

'Cut!'

Rani felt her heart rise as she saw the girl about to kiss the screen legend and she felt it fall as she realised their lips were not actually going to touch. There was a round of applause from the cast and crew who were watching the filming.

'We'll print that,' shouted the director. 'Set up for the next scene, make-up, do something about her hair!' he screamed at no one in particular. George came back to stand behind Rani's chair.

'And that's how it goes, all day long! Mr Khan stands about looking handsome, the girls faint into his arms and then they have a song and a dance.'

Rani began to laugh. 'You really know your Bollywood movies, don't you, George?' she said.

'Well, they do seem a bit formulaic, if you don't mind me saying, miss.'

'That's the way we like them.' It was Omar Khan. He'd made his way behind the camera and had crept up on them both without them noticing. Both George and Rani were startled.

'No offence, sir,' said George apologetically. 'I didn't

mean your films,' he stuttered as he tried to climb out of the hole he'd dug for himself.

'Mine are the *worst* offenders, George, you know that!' Omar laughed and patted the burly minder across the back. George looked relieved.

'Do you really think that, Mr Khan?' Rani asked.

'I thought I told you to call me Omar,' he said, crouching down so he was level with Rani.

'Close your eyes,' he ordered.

Rani was a little nervous and unsure if she should do as he commanded.

'Go on, close your eyes. It won't hurt, I promise,' he urged again with a smile that showed all of his trademark teeth and his penetrating eyes. Rather sheepishly Rani closed her eyes, scrunching them up tight in anticipation of what was going to happen. *Perhaps he's going to kiss me*, she thought. She felt the pounding of her heart again. And then the shock of something burning her ankle. She opened her eyes immediately and looked down.

'For you,' Omar said. 'They should help reduce the swelling.' Rani looked down to where her leg was supported by a small table and saw a bag of frozen peas sitting across her ankle.

'Peas!' she exclaimed with disappointment.

'Just so, peas—I said they'd help,' Omar said. 'I have to go now. George will take you back to town.' He turned to walk back to the set. 'I look forward to reading your interview, Miss de Silver,' he continued, and before Rani could think of a suitable reply he was gone.

'Peas,' she muttered in disgust. 'Peas, he gives me a bag of *matar*.' Rani turned to George. 'Can you take me home now, please? I think I'd like to go.'

Without saying anything George helped Rani up

and carried her all the way back to the limousine. The journey back to London was a quiet one. Rani was in a contemplative mood. Since she was a teenager she had looked up to the man in the posters, the handsome hero in the films and had imagined herself falling in love with him. Now she'd actually met him and it was true his eyes were a stunning colour and his body was powerfully built and oozed sex appeal. But there was something nagging at her. She'd wanted him to sweep her off her feet and instead he'd joked about her twisted ankle with all the sophistication of the school show-off. He'd made fun of her in front of other people. Peas, for God's sake—who was he trying to impress? Worse still, Rani felt stupid about her own feelings and told herself that she must stop daydreaming.

'George, what do you know about his mother?' She was thinking back to the photograph and the frame she'd broken.

'Nothing, miss.' George was happy to talk; he didn't like the silence.

'Have you ever met her?'

'No, miss. I'm not even sure she's still alive, to tell you the truth. He's, Mr Khan's, never mentioned her. I just know he likes 'aving her picture around the place.'

'You really know how to cheer a girl up, don't you?'

'Sorry, miss, I didn't mean it like that. Don't you worry, I've got it here,' he said, tapping a small bag on the passenger seat next to him, 'and I'll have her fixed before he even knows she's missing, so don't give it another thought.'

But she did. His mother had dark eyes in the photo, so Omar's beautiful green eyes must come from his father, Rani thought. Probably a Kashmiri. Not the sort of boy her mother would ever have let her play with when she'd been growing up! She was British-born, second generation, and her parents had taken advantage of every opportunity for her that they could. They had made sure she had a good education with ballet lessons and pony club and ski trips in the winter. Above everything else they had brought their only daughter up to know her own value and to know just what they expected from her. Dropping out of medical school was a shock her father was still getting over. He was in private practice himself and had naturally expected his daughter to follow him. After much persuasion by his wife he'd let her switch courses and had continued to fund her education, but it had tested their relationship and Rani knew it. *I'm a snob*, she thought to herself wryly. *No wonder I can't get a man—they're just not good enough!*

She looked out of the car window at the familiar landmarks; it was late afternoon, no point in going to the office.

'Would it be too much to ask for you to drop me off at my apartment, George?'

'No problem at all, miss. You just say where you want to go, George will do the rest.'

And he was true to his word. He drove Rani home and helped her into the flat. He was just leaving when Rani fired a shot straight at him that caught him off balance.

'George, I'm guessing Omar is a bit of a playboy—isn't he?'

George almost choked and his face began to fill up with blood as he struggled for an answer.

'He's had girlfriends, Miss Rani. A man does, doesn't he? You know—well, he would, wouldn't he? I mean—'

'I didn't mean to embarrass you, George.' Rani let

him off the hook by interrupting. 'I'm just curious. After all, he seems to enjoy being the centre of attention, the big star, doesn't he?'

'I'm really the wrong person to ask, miss.'

Rani realised she had gone too far and stepped back.

'I know I shouldn't have. I'm sorry, George. It puts you in an indelicate position, I suppose.'

'Not really that, miss. Just that I've been married almost thirty years, me and the missus, so I'm not the right sort to judge. Will that be all?'

'Just one other thing—what was all that nonsense in the car? You know, when I mentioned his dad and the book.' Rani smiled, hoping that would win her another constructive insight into Omar's world. 'It was like I'd just told him his granny was dead!'

George choked and tears began to run down his face. It grew red and hot and for a moment Rani thought she'd killed him.

'Are you OK? Can I get you some water?'

'I'll be fine.' George struggled to speak. 'Just a little shocked, that's all.'

'Sorry, George. Have I put my foot in it again?'

'No, no, no, it's quite all right, honestly.' His composure returned and George was able to continue. 'It's just that he can't stand his dad, hasn't seen him for years and now the book thing, well, it promises to be a stitch-up. You know the sort of thing—made-up stories and quotes to make Mr Khan look bad and paint his dad in a good light. You know, *"my son the millionaire and I'm living in squalor,"* sort of thing.'

'Only too well. Interesting, George, thanks for that, and thank you for looking after me. You're a lovely man. Your wife is a very lucky lady.'

Rani gave him a peck on the cheek as he left and

George began to get embarrassed again. *How do people stay married for so long?* she thought to herself with admiration as she watched George close the door.

Rani ran a bath, pouring in almost a bottle of bubble bath, put some bread into the toaster and filled the kettle. She needed to relax and she didn't know of a better way than having tea and toast sitting in the bath. While she waited for it to fill, she played her phone messages. There was one from her best friend, Sunita, another from her mother and several from the office. The last was from her editor, Tony, saying that she'd obviously fallen off the face of the planet because he'd been trying her mobile all day. Rani looked at the broken pieces of her phone and smiled; it had been rather nice to be out of touch. The message continued that because he hadn't heard from her, he was assuming everything had gone OK and could she send him the copy as soon as possible. She had an interview to write up but it could wait until she'd had a bath and some tea.

The water felt soothing as she slipped into the deep warm bath; the bubbles multiplied and slid over the side and tickled her nose. What a day! Rani wanted time to put her thoughts in order and this was just the place to do it. She closed her eyes and began to write her interview in her mind.

I have won the lottery, all my Christmases and birthdays are here at once, Vishnu is truly smiling down upon me. I'm finally face to face with the handsome vision of my dreams. And how does this reality manifest itself? With me lying flat on the pavement in a red party dress, a twisted ankle, staring up into his beautiful sparkling green eyes as the contents of my handbag roll into the gutter!

She was pleased with the start and felt so much better for the heat that was caressing her body.

Omar Khan stepped off the screen and out of my dreams; his hand outstretched, helping me to my feet. My hero! True to life but could the heart-throb keep up this kind of performance?

Rani felt the interview was really going to come together rather well, but she'd need her tape recorder and notes for a punchy quote. That would mean leaving the womblike sanctuary of the tub, which didn't please her. She slipped back beneath the bubbles, trying to put off the inevitable. But the phone rang again and she popped her head back up to listen to the message. It was the office yet again. A story had been pulled by the lawyers and they needed her interview with Omar Khan that evening for the Saturday edition. She had an hour to file the copy. Now she had no choice; she would have to get out of the bath.

There was something very satisfying about writing to a deadline. When it was reached there was nothing more to be done. Rani made another cup of tea and powered up her Mac. She began flipping through her shorthand notebook and rewound the tape recording she'd made. As the tea slipped down her throat she began to type. Her words flowed with the same satisfying warmth as the tea.

For twenty years Omar Khan has dominated our movies and our hearts. Still only thirty-eight, he is already one of the greatest of the Bollywood greats, mobbed by adoring fans wherever he goes, but still humble enough to carry an old battered photograph of his mother around with him.

For the next hour Rani pounded away on the keyboard of her computer, occasionally stopping to turn a page in her notebook or to take a sip of tea.

'Yuk!' she exclaimed as she took a cold mouthful from the mug and spat it back in shock. She paused to reread what she had written and her hand went to her mouth as she bit her lip.

'My God, this looks like I fancy him,' she said out loud as her eyes darted along the lines of her story. She frantically created a new file and began rewriting it. She was conscious of the time now and knew that at any moment her office would call demanding she file the story. Her fingers furiously darted across the keys, making sure that this time it didn't sound as if she had fallen in love with him! When she felt happy she wrote a quick email and attached the document; it flew from her fingers and away to the office.

Rani slumped back in her chair and put her hands to her face. She felt hot; her cheeks were burning. What was that? The anxiety of having to meet the deadline? No, she'd been up against those many times before. Perhaps it was meeting a megastar that she'd had a girlish crush on? Perhaps. Or was it what she had originally written about him? She clicked on her documents file and pulled out the first draft and began rereading it. The burning in her cheeks grew as she went over the words again. Rani could feel the heat move to her chest. She pulled her dressing gown apart and saw the telltale red flush across her breasts and quickly closed it, embarrassed by her own intense feelings. She got up from the computer and walked around the apartment in an effort to cool down.

'Thank God I changed it,' she said to the empty flat. 'I need more tea,' and then, 'Why am I talking to myself?' she continued as she paced to and fro around the boiling kettle. Clearly the legendary film star had got to her in a way she didn't think either of them had thought possible. The ringing of the phone stopped Rani contemplating her emotions any further. This time she managed to answer it.

'Great stuff with Omar Khan, Rani!' It was Tony. 'Really good quotes and a very nice turn of phrase. I've just finished looking at it and it's off to lay-up now so we'll get it in for tomorrow.'

'Thanks, Tony, it was quite a day,' Rani replied cautiously.

'Sounds like it! Really, it's great work, you've obviously thrown yourself into it and I loved the bit about the broken mobile.' He began to chuckle. 'But do me a favour, please, Rani—get yourself a back-up phone next time. Getting hold of you was like raising the dead! Any way I've gotta go, thanks again, you've got us out of a jam. Have a good weekend.' And he was gone as quickly as he'd begun his call.

Rani was a little taken aback. She'd never had so much praise from her boss before. She went back to her tea making and then headed to bed. She was worn out, physically and emotionally; it really had been quite a day.

It was the singing that finally woke Rani the following morning. She thought she'd been dreaming it but it wouldn't go away and eventually, begrudgingly, she got out of bed to see who it was.

'I'm coming, I'm coming,' she said as she trudged towards the door, her ankle still giving her some pain, although it was much better today—probably due to those peas, she thought with a wry smile. She could hear voices on the other side. It was her best friends

Sunita and Shilpa and they were singing 'Happy Birthday' to her.

'Come on, let us in, birthday girl,' said Sunita.

'Yes, hurry up, Rani!' added Shilpa.

'What is it? Has Armani launched a range of designer kameez?' Rani retorted as she opened the door. Her two friends were grinning like Cheshire cats.

'Happy birthday, Rani. What have you got to say for yourself, young lady?' Sunita questioned. She was waving a copy of the morning's *London Review.* Shilpa was clutching a bag of presents. Rani looked and felt bemused.

'What are you on about?' she asked with genuine concern. Shilpa and Sunita looked at each other, shrugged their shoulders and then looked back at Rani.

'You, you minx! Gushing all over Omar Khan. I'm surprised you didn't ask him to marry you!' said Shilpa. The penny dropped and Rani finally understood what they were going on about.

'My interview, I see, very funny, ha, ha,' she said. 'It wasn't that bad.' The girls looked at each other again and Sunita began to quote from the paper she held.

'"I was weak with excitement as he touched my hand, this handsome hunk of a man, this demigod, and here was I breathing the air that he had exhaled."'

'Need I go on?' asked Sunita.

'Oh, my God, they've printed the wrong version!' Rani exclaimed. She went bright red and her heart raced and her fingers went into her mouth. She turned from her friends and ran back into her flat to her computer. Frantically she began searching through her sent emails and then let out a little gasp in shock. She'd attached the original draft, not her rewritten one!

'Rani, Rani, what is it, *didi*?' Sunita said as she followed her friend into the living room.

Sunita put a comforting arm around her friend's shoulders.

'There, there, it will be OK,' she said, not knowing what else to say.

'She doesn't remember what she's written—that's an age thing, that is. Don't worry. We've all known you've fancied him for years and now you've told him—a bold move, I must say!' exclaimed Shilpa as she stood at the doorway. Sunita waved her hand, shooing her away.

'You don't understand,' Rani cried in a muffled voice.

'Don't understand what? That you fancy a Bollywood hunk? What's not to understand? You go for it!' Shilpa said, she couldn't help herself, but, realising she'd overstepped the mark, she backed away. Sunita put her head next to Rani's.

'What won't we understand?' she said in a caring voice. Rani continued to sob.

'Shilpa's right, I've fancied him for years and look what happens when I meet him. I twist my ankle and gush like a stupid girl!' She paused, turning her head to her friend. The crying had made her eyes red and the tears were still flowing down her cheeks.

'It may sound really stupid,' she continued in a stuttering voice, 'it sounds stupid to me as I'm saying it, but I felt a connection between us.' She paused for a moment. 'Like, like when I met David.'

That was a name none of them had spoken for several years and it was enough to stop the clocks from ticking.

'Tea, anyone?' Shilpa put her head round the door from the kitchen and peered in. *Sorry*, she mouthed at

Rani. Rani nodded her acceptance of the apology and took the tea.

'That's a great idea,' said Sunita, trying to lighten the mood a little more, 'and then you can tell us all about it. You've started now so you have to!'

They sat on the sofas in the living room, each nursing a mug of tea, and Rani began recounting the events of the previous twenty-four hours. Sunita and Shilpa weren't bystanders and kept interrupting her.

'When he picked you up from the pavement, how did it feel?' asked Shilpa, her eyes wide with excitement.

'Like I'd been plugged into an electric socket! I felt completely weak all over my body, like I was going to pass out or something.'

'Tell us about his eyes,' questioned Sunita.

'Oh, yes, yes, Rani, what were his eyes like? Are they really as deep and green as they seem on the screen?' Shilpa added her request, anxious to know every little detail. Rani nodded.

'Greener and more stunning than you can imagine. I thought I would drown in them. They were as crystal clear, as rich as the finest Sri Lankan emeralds.' Rani began to lay it on for the benefit of her friends. But inside she was reliving the moments as she retold the story and as she spoke she felt warm from the inside of her body to the surface of her skin.

'He was everything you would want him to be,' she added, but stopped, unsure of what she was going to say next.

'But,' said Sunita. 'You were going to say something more and there was a *"but,"* wasn't there?'

'Oh, you know me too well,' Rani said, picking up a cushion and throwing it at Sunita.

'So go on, then, don't leave us in suspense—what is

it?' asked Shilpa as she shifted in her seat. Rani sighed before continuing.

'As I sat watching them film a scene of the movie he came up to me and asked me to close my eyes. He said he had a surprise for me.'

'I bet he did!' exclaimed Shilpa and began to giggle. Sunita threw a cushion at her.

'Well, I didn't know what to expect and I was nervous. I thought perhaps he was going to kiss me. But instead he put a bag of frozen peas on my ankle!'

'How disappointing!' Shilpa said, biting her lip.

'You see, there was...' she hesitated '...there *is* something about him, I'm sure there is, and I know I don't know him but I feel like I do so I wrote it down...' Rani suddenly groaned out loud and clutched her head with her hands. 'What if he reads it? Oh, my God, I'll just die!' she said as her voice reached a level of panic the others had never witnessed. She grabbed a cushion and buried her face in it.

'So what if he reads it?' Sunita said supportively. 'You're a journalist—journalists make stuff up all the time to sell papers, don't they? So, then, where's the harm? He's just another interview you've done, that's all.'

'But what will your mum think?' asked Shilpa pointedly. 'I mean, he's not exactly take-home-and-meet-the-parents material, is he? Well, not your mum and dad anyway! I mean, he's a flashy actor, not a respectable doctor, isn't he?'

Rani rolled her eyes but Shilpa continued, 'He's not even a lawyer! He's a song and dance man, and you know your father really wouldn't approve, especially if he'd read any of the newspaper cuttings. His only daughter mixed up with an international playboy!'

'Aaahh,' screamed Rani in sheer frustration. 'I'll die of shame! I'll move house, I'll move city, I'll move country!' she yelled. The phone rang. It was the duty editor from her office. Rani let the answer phone cut in.

'Rani? It's Edward Evans here, just thought you'd like to know we've had a tremendous response to your interview with Omar Khan. Never seen anything like it: the punters love it; the website has crashed; we've had so many people trying to leave messages. They're calling you an Asian Bridget Jones. Great stuff. And I'm sure Tony will be in touch—he's as bowled over as the rest of us.'

'Bridget Jones!' Sunita said. 'That chain-smoking, alcoholic, man-obsessed thirty-something?'

'I don't smoke, I hardly drink and I'm exactly twenty-five today!' Rani protested.

'So you admit to being man-obsessed, then?' Shilpa chipped in cheekily.

The doorbell rang.

'What now?' Rani said almost hysterically. 'Please can you get it?' she begged, looking towards her friends. Sunita obliged and headed towards the door. Rani and Shilpa could hear a conversation but couldn't make any of it out. Sunita returned, smiling across her face and holding a very large display of flowers out in front of her.

'I think you can afford to relax now,' said Sunita. 'These are from him,' she said, plonking the impressive display down onto the coffee table. 'Here, take a look at the note that came with them.' She handed it to Rani. 'The delivery man said they were ordered first thing this morning.' Rani opened the little envelope and began to read.

'I enjoyed your article, Rani. Peas be upon you. Omar.'

'What does he mean *"peas"*?' asked Shilpa, who was frowning at the display.

'They're sweet peas, the flowers—he's sent hundreds of sweet peas,' said Rani, beginning to laugh. Shilpa still looked confused.

'The frozen peas?' said Sunita, hoping it would trigger a connection for Shilpa. 'Remember? He put a bag of frozen peas on Rani's ankle—well, this is another pea joke.'

'Oh,' said Shilpa. 'Taking the peas, more like,' and they all fell about laughing. They were wiping tears from their eyes when there was another knock at the door.

'I'll get it,' said an enthusiastic Shilpa, jumping to her feet. There was a short exchange of words and she returned holding a small silver tray in one hand.

'For you,' she said, bending down and offering it to Rani. Sunita crowded in to see what it was.

'I bet it's from him again,' she said.

'Oh, he's so smooth,' Shilpa said as she sighed. Rani was tearing the envelope open as fast as her nervous fingers could manage. There was a small card inside and a short handwritten note. She read it to herself.

'Come on—what does it say?' urged an eager Shilpa.

'He wants to see me again,' Rani said. There was a slight tremor in her voice. 'He says he hopes I liked the little joke, which he couldn't resist, and would I like to be his guest at the opening of his new club tonight.'

'Tonight!' exclaimed Shilpa. 'He's not wasting any time, is he? And you thought you might put him off by throwing yourself at his feet. Looks like he can't keep away!'

CHAPTER TWO

OMAR WAS SITTING alone in his bedroom. After the previous day's filming George had driven him to the country house in Hertfordshire that was his home in England. It was a large sprawling place and cost a fortune to maintain. But he didn't need to worry about the money. Since his career had taken off Omar never bothered to check his bank account. He just bought what he fancied and let his accountant take care of the bills. He had more money than he'd ever dreamed about while living in that dingy two-roomed flat with his father. Even now, after all the years that had gone by, he gritted his teeth when he thought back to those days. The anger had never left him.

Now he was surrounded by works of art by people he'd never heard of, objects of luxury he certainly never needed, but he'd bought because he could. They showed the outside world that he had made it to the big time and he liked that. It was just part of showing off, of playing the role of the superstar. It was his way of sticking a finger up to all the people who'd ever done him wrong or who looked down their noses at him because they felt they were better than him. So what if they were? He had the money to rub in their faces and, coming from a poor background, he knew one thing for certain—money could buy you power.

But was he truly happy? He hadn't really given it much thought. He'd got on with playing the role of the celebrity film star, attending the parties, being photographed with gorgeous women. He couldn't help but think that, for all he was surrounded by the outward signs of wealth, his bed was often cold when he got in it at night.

'George, George,' Omar called out. 'Any word from that reporter?' George made his way up the stairs from the ground floor. He was puffing.

'Not a thing.'

'Huh!' Omar said. 'Ah, well, some you win, some you lose, eh!' He tried to shrug off the disappointment he felt by making a joke of it. 'Shame; she could have really helped me out—she's just what I need at the moment—but I'm sure we can find someone else. We better had—the publishers are nagging me about the book. Pity, it would have saved a lot of time and effort and she is very, very pretty.' He looked at George. George didn't respond.

'Unlike you to hold back on giving me your opinion, especially if I don't want it,' Omar commented dryly. George remained tight-lipped. 'Oh, come on, George! What did you think of her? She liked you, didn't she?' He threw the paper towards the silent George. 'Here, read what she put about you again. *"Courteous and charming, George the driver is always there to lend a hand."*' George began to blush.

'She's certainly different to all the others, sir.'

Omar was just about to question what George meant, but his manservant continued, 'We should be going soon. The opening is at eight and you know what the traffic will be like.'

'Oh, don't mother me, George! Fashionably late, you know it's my way. Anyway, it's my club. I'll turn up when I like!'

The noise of the club hit them head-on as they ran from the cover of the limousine and through the crowd waiting in the rain to get in. The burly, stone-faced doormen nodded as the three women zoomed past laughing and giggling. The lobby was brightly lit with huge palms on either side of a magnificent marble staircase. The guests were being ushered up it by smiling hostesses bearing trays of champagne. Rani and her friends ignored them and made straight for the top of the stairs. Their high heels chinked with each step. Sunita stopped and took a glass of champagne from a waiter at the top of the staircase, turned to Rani and began to sing 'Happy Birthday'.

Shilpa joined in, laughing all the way through the verse as everyone turned to look at them.

'Happy birthday, dear Rani, happy birthday to you!' There was a round of applause from the onlookers and Rani flushed red.

'Oh, my God! And you had to tell the whole club!' she said, giving Sunita a tight hug and kiss on her cheek.

'Well, it's only once a year and we need to celebrate, don't we, Bridget?'

They linked arms and marched into the club as if it were them that owned it and not Omar Khan. There was something totally liberating about being old enough not to care what other people thought but young enough to still get the looks and they still did. Every man's head turned as the three beautiful women walked through the double doors and into the main bar. As soon as they stepped inside the first man willing to chance his luck approached them. He was tall and dark-haired, wearing a sharp suit and a tie in a thick Windsor knot. He made straight for Rani.

'Good evening, gorgeous. Would you like a drink?'

She smiled politely and shook her head. 'We're fine, thanks.' She continued to walk towards the bar.

'Who's the *gora*?' asked Sunita.

'I've never seen him before,' Rani replied with a wide smile. They hadn't been in the club five minutes and they were already being admired. It felt good but she was very anxious. Her friends had talked her into accepting the invitation to the opening of Omar Khan's club and she'd reluctantly agreed just hours before.

'I'm not sure I can face him again, not after what I've written about him, and knowing he's read it.'

'Look,' said Sunita, 'think about it this way, he wouldn't have invited you if he was upset, would he? He knows just how you feel about him, doesn't he?'

'The whole world does!' said Shilpa.

'What I mean,' Sunita began again, 'is that he knows you.'

'He knows he's onto a good thing!' Shilpa butted in before Sunita could finish what she was going to say.

'I wasn't going to put it quite like that,' said Sunita, 'but he does know you're interested in him—so what? It's about time you looked forward and not back.'

'That's just what I'm afraid of,' said Rani. 'I'm not like that—you know that.'

'You know you mentioned the D word this morning?' Sunita probed, hoping to excavate a little more of the truth.

Rani looked shocked. She'd brought up David?

'I did?' she questioned her friends. They both nodded.

'You see, that's why I'm scared. I mean, I would never have said…that…I mean…really, would I? You know…it's…' Rani struggled to express herself. 'If I got involved with Omar, what if it was like it was with David all over again? I mean, imagine how awful that would be.'

Sunita looked straight into Rani's eyes.

'He sent you flowers, didn't he? Why did he invite you to his club? It's not out of charity, is it? He could have any woman he wants, can't he?'

'That really makes me feel special, that does!' baulked Rani.

'You know I didn't mean it like that,' said Sunita. 'It's just that he's obviously interested or why go to all the effort?'

'You won't find out unless you go,' said Shilpa.

'For once I agree with her,' said Sunita. 'You've got to be in it to win it, as they say, so come on—you've nothing to lose.'

'My dignity, my self-respect,' pointed out Rani.

'You lost that the moment you hit the send key on your computer.' Shilpa laughed.

'But I feel too embarrassed to face him. What will I say? What can I say?' Rani asked, her face stricken with worry. Her two friends now sat either side of her, each with an arm around her waist.

'You don't have to say *anything*,' said Sunita. 'You just have to be you. Go on, enjoy yourself. After all, it's not every day a Bollywood superstar asks you out, is it? And anyway, you can just brush it off as journalistic exaggeration, can't you? What's the worst that could happen?' Sunita continued.

'She could get pregnant, that's the worst!' said Shilpa and then, putting on a matriarchal Indian accent, 'Beti, you make sure he's a good man, an honest man.' She was wagging her finger at Rani like a scolding mother. 'Make sure he's handsome, make sure he loves you, make sure he's a doctor. And, if he's none of these, make sure he's rich!' They all hugged and laughed.

'Come on, then, no time to lose,' said Sunita.

Rani had met Sunita on their first day at university. They'd been allocated rooms next door to each other in the halls of residence and had struck up an immediate friendship that hadn't wavered in the subsequent years. They'd even started out on the same course, medicine—what else for two Asian girls? But Rani had grown frustrated by the length of time it was going to take to finish, and, much against her parents' advice, dropped out to study journalism instead. That was what she'd told her parents anyway. But it wasn't the truth; she'd never been able to open her heart to them about the real reasons for switching course. She was too scared to admit it even now, but the unpleasant memories of that ordeal were stirring deep inside Rani's stomach again. She was trying her best to ignore them and she knew it. The self-deception was paper thin because no matter how she tried to distract herself it was always there at the back of her mind and in her aching tummy. David. That one word that summed up her entire attitude and experience of men. One word that caused a tower block of feelings to crash in on itself. One word she'd not uttered since leaving university. One word that encapsulated all of the extremes of love and pain, just five little letters. David was the real reason Rani had dropped out of medical school. He had said he loved her. She had thought she loved him. He cast a long shadow over Rani and meeting Omar had brought back all of those memories and they tore at her now.

The rest of the day was spent in preparation for the night out. There was plenty of discussion and squabbling about what to wear. How to do Rani's hair and what make-up was appropriate.

'You don't want to look tarty,' Shilpa advised. 'Go with the gold. It says, I'm sophisticated and know my own value.' Rani and Sunita looked amazed.

'An eyeliner can tell you all that?' asked Rani.

'Of course! Don't you girls know anything? No wonder you're both single.'

'And you're not?' Rani retorted. Shilpa ignored the comment and continued to extol the virtues of her make-up choice. Sunita helped Rani with her eyebrows, expertly shaping them with thread. Shilpa offered to give Rani a wax but she declined. Instead she took charge of the curlers and began to set Rani's long brown hair.

'He's a film star, he's used to perfection, so we've got to give you the film-star look,' she said, rolling strands of hair up. The day passed in a blur of colour and conversation as Rani paraded her entire wardrobe and they discussed the merits of each outfit. Apart from some family occasions the opportunities to wear traditional clothes were rare and they all made the most of the preparations for Rani's big night out.

'What about this?' Rani said as she tried on a marigold-yellow churidaar pjama.

'Nah, too bright. It's not a ladies' sangeet, you know!' replied Sunita. She busied herself rummaging through

Rani's impressive jewellery cabinet and laid the pieces on the bed. There were simple plain gold chains, wonderful solid bracelets and her prized possession, her panjagla given to her by her mother as a hint that she should be looking for a husband. In the end Rani decided on her black halter-neck sari, which was decorated with waves of silver sequins and embroidered flowers.

Now they were actually in the club Rani felt nervous about meeting Omar again. Just what would she say to him? What could she say that would undo the embarrassment she felt? She breathed in deeply and vowed to enjoy herself whatever else happened that night. The club was bright and cheerful with a dance floor to the left and low tables with comfortable-looking cream sofas on the right. The wall behind the bar was lined with hundreds of different bottles and the staff seemed to know which ones they were picking up without even looking. A waiter wearing a very tight pair of trousers came out from the side of the bar.

'Ladies, good evening, welcome to The Palace. Your table's this way. Mr Khan knows you have arrived,' he said, and they followed him to an empty table behind the dance floor. Rani's heart skipped at the mention of his name and she began to think the whole idea was a huge mistake. They sat down and as the waiter turned to ask them what they'd like to drink Sunita had a fit of the giggles.

'Where do you think he puts his tips?' she whispered, looking at his tight trousers. Her laughter was infectious and Rani began to giggle too.

'Not in his shorts, that's for sure!' she said. They hadn't even finished ordering their drinks when the music began. It was Beyoncé.

'Come on, let's dance,' said Shilpa, and the three of them headed to the dance floor, leaving the waiter still hanging on for their order. Rani loved to dance and it felt great being with her best friends. She felt safe on the hard wooden dance floor, as if it were her own private island, a place where all the things she was afraid of couldn't get to her. A sanctuary in a sea of confusion she was anxious about swimming in. But the tranquillity didn't last. Rani's nose twitched. It was definitely his aftershave. She spun around to find Omar standing beside her.

'Very stylish. You dance well,' he said. 'Can I?' and he put his arms out to hold her hands and dance. Rani was in a state of shock and just instinctively let him take hold and spin her away from her friends.

'I'm glad you were able to make it,' he said, leaning in towards Rani's ear. His breath felt warm and intimate on her skin as they glided around the dance floor. 'I wasn't sure you'd got the messages.'

Rani felt guilty. She hadn't responded to the flowers or the invitation and was about to try and explain when Omar continued as if he sensed she was backed into a corner.

'The doormen spotted you as you came in. All the staff had been given a photograph of you, just in case.'

Rani felt relieved and affronted at the same time. He obviously cared enough to have everyone look out for her, but at the same time she felt vulnerable being identified like that to people she didn't know.

'Do you make a habit of spying on women?'

'No, but in your case I'm happy to make an exception.'

Well, at least he's honest about it, Rani thought to herself wryly. *And he does move very well!* She let him lead her around the dance floor, trying not to get too carried away.

'How's the ankle?' he asked with genuine concern in his voice.

'Much better, thank you. I didn't have any peas at home, but oven chips work just as well.' That made Omar laugh out loud.

'You're a very funny lady.'

Rani felt a little put out by the description. Funny! Like ha-ha, or odd to look at? she wondered.

'Funny? In what way?'

Omar looked straight into her eyes and she could feel the intensity of them frazzle her mind.

'In a good way. I mean, saying that about the chips, and the way you wrote about me. I like your sense of humour. It's very attractive.'

Rani gulped at his directness. He wasn't like any of the men her mum and dad had paraded in front of her in an effort to find her a husband. They had all been well-mannered doctors, dentists or lawyers who knew which knife and fork to use and when. They wouldn't have been caught running their eyes up and down her body, and if they had they'd at least have had the decency to be embarrassed.

'That's a little forward, don't you think?' Rani said in her most cut-glass accent.

'And then you spoil it by being so snobby,' Omar said in his roughest Mancunian delivery.

Rani pushed Omar away with a haughty snort, but he still had hold of her hands and pulled her back towards him with little effort. She crashed into his chest and he held her tightly against his body, squeezing her breasts against his silk shirt.

'Are you really as toffee-nosed as you seem, Ms de Silver?' His eyes burned into her.

'Let's finish dancing first and I'll let you know,' Rani said, giving up the struggle to be free from his muscular grip. Her stomach was spinning with the sheer exhilaration of being so close to him and being so powerless. She wanted to pull away and at the same time wanted to know what it would feel like to be crushed against his bare skin. As they moved gently to the next song Rani knew just what the experience reminded her of. She felt like a cartoon character with a good angel on one shoulder and a naughty devil on the other. So far she thought the mischievous, impish side was winning and she liked it. No wonder her mother had disapproved of the posters of Omar on her bedroom wall. What would she think of her now? Rani let her face fall closer to his and breathed in his aftershave again. His stubble tickled her cheek but she didn't flinch away; she savoured the feeling.

As Omar moved cautiously he could feel her heart beating so near to his and he wondered how much closer he could hold her. He was in a playful mood, enjoying the sensation of Rani's chest pressed against his. She had a lovely smile and, as far as he could tell, a very shapely body. As Rani relaxed in his grip he slowly let his hands slide down the sides of her black sari until his left hand was supporting her shoulder blades and his right hand was in the small of her back just above the curve of her bottom.

'Why don't we have that drink now?' Rani said in a rushed tone, twisting her body away from Omar's. Just as Rani stretched their arms as far as they could go without actually letting go Omar tugged her back towards him like a yo-yo, spinning her back into his arms.

It was so quick that Rani didn't have time to resist as he bent his head low towards her mouth and planted a kiss on her lips. Her eyes were wide open as she stared in shock up into his, and then as his lips gently moved against hers she closed her eyes and let him kiss her.

'Champagne!' Omar declared, releasing her suddenly. Taking hold of Rani's right hand, he led her towards his private table away from the main bar.

'Wow, what was that for?' Rani asked as she regained some of her composure.

'The kiss? Because I wanted to. Didn't you?' Omar asked with a wide grin breaking over his face. 'Come on, have a glass with me. I've something to say to you.' And he sat down patting the sofa next to him. Rani sat beside him and took the drink.

'Happy birthday.'

'You knew!' Rani was surprised and pleased.

'Of course. These things are important. But I have another motive for getting you alone.'

Rani's eyes widened with anticipation. Omar smiled.

'Do you know anyone who's any good at ghostwriting autobiographies?' he said. 'You must have come across someone in your line of business.'

It wasn't what Rani had expected, but then she wasn't sure what to expect; even in the short time she'd known him it was hard to second-guess what was going to happen next. Omar continued.

'You see, I've been approached to write my autobiography. The publishers are very keen but I haven't got a clue where to start.'

'How about at the beginning?' Rani suggested as Omar's words were finally sinking in. 'Or perhaps with a key event in your life.' She paused for a moment as she regained her thoughts and her journalistic nose sniffed a story. 'How about the day you landed your first major role, or when you moved to Pakistan, perhaps something to do with your mother or father?'

Omar visibly twitched at the mention of his parents but he didn't say anything to deflect the point.

'You see, you're full of the right sort of ideas. I knew you'd be able to help. You're just the woman to ask.' He took a sip from his glass. 'Whoever helped me would be well paid; the publisher has offered a very agreeable advance. But they need it like yesterday, they want to run it as a spoiler to *that other book*.' He spat the words out and the venom with which he addressed the forthcoming book by his own father wasn't lost on Rani.

'A spoiler, eh?' she mused.

'Yes, just what is that?' he asked.

'Oh, we use them all the time. If we know a big story or interview is going to be published in another paper we try and cobble something together and rush it out before our rivals. It's pretty much par for the course in our business.'

Omar's eyes widened.

'Any idea how long they want it to be?' she asked.

'I haven't got a clue, but they keep calling me wanting to know my thoughts and suggestions and who might ghost-write it for me, so, if you can think of anyone suitable, the money's good.'

'I'm sure it's a good deal. I'll have a think for you.' But she was already wondering why she had let herself be bullied into accepting his invitation by her so-called friends and why she felt herself falling for his good looks yet again. And how she could convince him that she was the right woman for the job. She gave a little shake of her head. *You see, even when you are angry with him you are thinking how to spend more time with him*, she said to herself. *You're a hopeless case, Rani de Silver!*

'Are you OK?' Omar asked.

'I'm fine, thank you. I've had a lovely evening. But I really must get back to my friends,' she said, standing up. 'I've ignored them for far too long.' Her head was spinning. Perhaps it was the champagne; after all, she wasn't really much of a drinker. *Yes, that's it. It must be the bubbles*, Rani said to herself as she stumbled away from Omar, the scent of his aftershave still lingering in her nostrils.

'Think about what I said,' he called after her. 'I mean it.'

Rani fanned herself with her hand, trying to cool herself down. She was hot and flustered and felt an ache in her stomach, as if she had just denied herself something very naughty, like a tub of ice cream, and she had. As she arrived back at her own table Shilpa was tapping her watch.

'You remembered us, then?' Shilpa said jokily. 'I thought we wouldn't see you for days.' Rani collapsed between them. Sunita turned towards her.

'So tell us all about it, everything, every detail, don't you dare miss anything out,' she pestered.

Shilpa raised her eyebrows in a teasing and questioning way. 'Did he proposition you?'

'Oh, Shilpa!' said Sunita.

'Well, I was only asking!'

Rani smiled at her, shaking her head. Shilpa looked more disappointed. 'See, Sunita,' Shilpa said, 'I was telling you he was too old. I bet he can't even manage it, not at his age. You know people would stare at you in the streets, don't you? The age gap, of course. They'd think you were his daughter or his carer or something.' Rani and Sunita looked aghast.

'Have you finished?' Rani said sternly. Shilpa nodded.

'Thank you! He's not even forty! And you know very well that I'm not that sort of girl! Actually he's got a job he wants doing,' Rani said.

'Doing what? Chewing his food or wiping his saggy old bottom! I say good riddance. He wasn't good enough for you anyway!' Shilpa retorted.

'As a matter of fact he wants someone to ghost-write his autobiography for him.'

'Wow, that really is a job,' said Sunita.

'Impressive,' said Shilpa, 'I always said he was the man for you!'

Omar pulled his gold-plated phone from inside his jacket and turned it on with a sliding thumb. He scrolled down his recent calls and touched the number he was after. While he waited for the call to be answered he finished off the glass of champagne on the small table in front of him and poured another one.

'Hello, Spencer, it's me. I think I've got just the person, or should I say woman, to ghost-write my book. Yes, she is very attractive. As it happens I've just been having a drink with her. I'm sure she'll be fine. Legs? Yes, they go all the way up! No, I won't go and take a photo of her for you. You're supposed to be my lawyer, not a pervert checking up on the women I date. Anyway, it's not like that.' He paused for a moment and a sip of champagne. 'Well, I don't think it is. Anyway, can you let the publishers know and work up some sort of airtight confidentiality contract she'll have to sign? The last thing I need is another kiss-and-tell story breaking in the papers. Thanks.'

As he ended the call Omar was still thinking about Rani. She'd quite literally fallen into his life at just the moment he needed someone who could write. Perhaps it was fate or more likely coincidence. Either way it was very fortuitous and she was beautiful. He'd enjoyed the kiss he'd stolen from her and he realised that he actually felt guilty about it. That was a first.

He relaxed back into the leather sofa and took another glug of champagne. He was very pleased with himself for the neatness of the solution and the bonus of working with a good-looking ghost writer was just that, a bonus. Plenty had been written about him over the years, and some of it had actually been true. One thing he knew for certain was, the further he'd moved away from his upbringing, the more protective of his past he'd become. He couldn't figure that out but it was true—he had become almost obsessed with the notion of discovery. That other people shouldn't know about his life before he was an international superstar. He'd built a career on being an action hero and didn't like the idea that he'd been anything other than that. Any book by his father was bound to burst the bubbles of illusion that he'd created by being so famous for so long.

After all, his name had been linked to some of the most attractive women in the world—what would it say to his fans if they discovered he'd been brought up over a fish and chip shop in a dodgy part of Manchester? That he was normal and just like them? He didn't want to be normal. He didn't want to be like the millions of people who crammed into cinemas to see his latest movie. He liked the separation, he liked the feeling of being on a pedestal that fame and money had brought him. Above all he liked not having any of his inadequacies on display. Money could buy you that sort of privacy and the world would never have to know you didn't have many educational qualifications or know exactly where you had come from. Control the past so you could control the future—that was the way to succeed, so he had to make sure he got his own side of the story out to counter whatever his father was publishing. In that respect, Rani could be his saviour.

CHAPTER THREE

THERE WAS A knock on the door. It was George.

'Good morning, miss,' he called through the letter-box. 'Sorry to disturb you but I've been sent by Mr Khan. He wanted to know if you would like to join him for brunch.'

Rani thought she must be hearing things. Surely no self-respecting person got out of bed this early on a Sunday morning? Especially if they'd been out the night before celebrating their birthday. She quickly pulled on her dressing gown and headed to the door.

'Hello, George,' she said as she opened it, beckoning him in. He stepped cautiously inside the flat, wiping his feet several times before moving from the door.

'Is this for real, George?'

'Yes, miss, he woke me up before six and sent me over, in case you went out or anything.'

Rani was still coming to terms with the time of the day and had switched into automatic mode, filling the kettle, getting cups ready for tea.

'Tea?' she asked George.

'If it's not too much trouble, that would be lovely. I'm parched, miss.'

'Poor George, he treats you like a slave!'

George blushed and protested at the same time.

'Not at all, miss. All part of the job, isn't it? Twenty-four-hour service if he wants it.'

Rani made a pot of tea and then headed back to her bedroom.

'I'll be out in a minute. Help yourself to the tea when you think it's brewed enough for you.' She ran the shower and climbed in. The water refreshed her face as it hit it. Two minutes later she was back in the living room sipping from a cup of tea. George stood with his back to the wall, rather embarrassed by the situation.

'What do you think I should do, George?'

The question came out of the blue and struck George between the eyes and completely unaware. He almost dropped his cup.

'Hardly my place to say, miss, is it, really?'

'That's a fair point. Perhaps I shouldn't have asked you. It's just that you know him a lot better than me and, well, I thought you might have some advice for a girl in distress!' She smiled with her eyes at George.

'You know that's not fair, miss. But it's only brunch, isn't it, so where's the harm?'

He has a point, thought Rani. *Nothing can happen if I don't want it to, can it? So where is the harm?*

'OK, it's a deal. Give me five minutes and I'll be ready.' Rani disappeared back into her bedroom to finish getting dressed. Ten minutes later they were driving away from the flat. Rani looked up towards her apartment with a sense of excitement tinged with nervous anticipation. Her mother would be calling in an hour and there would be nobody in to answer the phone. That made Rani smile mischievously.

'So where are we heading to, George?'

'We're heading to Hertfordshire, miss, shouldn't be too long. The boss has a very nice place out there. You just sit back and relax. If you want anything just buzz me.' And he gave a wink, which Rani saw in the mirror. She hadn't known him long but she knew George was one of the good guys.

Well, here I am again, she said to herself as they drove out of the capital and onto the motorway. *It's madness; I've been living my life in a whirlwind and it really needs to slow down.*

Rani pulled a small notebook out of her handbag and drew a line down the centre of one page. At the top of one column she wrote *For*, at the top of the other she wrote *Against*. She began listing. Wonderful smile, amazing eyes, change of scene, opportunity, all came under the *For* column. Under the *Against* column she wrote: 'my mum and dad, his accent, manners, insecurity, the age difference'. She began to chew the end of the pen she was writing with, mulling over the meaning and implication of each word she added to either of the columns. Without realising what she was writing next she added the word 'David' to the list. She had put it under the *For* column and then immediately added it below the *Against* list. What she had hoped would be a way of helping her make her mind up just became a very long list of things that she could worry about.

She closed the book and put it away, looking out of the window for inspiration or a sign of some sort. There was nothing except the countryside, rolling hills soon giving way to pasture and fields of cows and wheat. There was the unmistakable smell from brightly coloured rapeseed that seemed to have been planted in every other field. *If that's the smell of the country*, she thought, *you can keep it*! George's voice came through on the intercom.

'Almost there now, miss. Can you see that wood to

the right? Well, it's a little way past there. We'll be turning off down more of those country roads you like so much.'

'Thanks for the warning,' Rani said. The knots in her stomach that had been there each time she'd been close to Omar began to tie themselves again. Her pulse increased and her breathing quickened. The closer they got to their destination, the worse it got.

'Just another half-mile, Miss de Silver,' George said. That was the first time he'd used her surname, Rani noticed. There was no disguising the house. They had made their way along a single-track road that suddenly broadened into an avenue of trees. They seemed to go on for ever in a gentle curve to the right and as they approached the bend Rani saw the house. It was an impressive solid-stone Georgian mansion. Rani counted the windows. There were twelve smaller ones in the top row and then two more rows of much larger windows below. Again, twelve in each. There was no mistaking the entrance, which was a stone canopy supported by four large pillars on either side. The car crunched along the gravel drive as George pulled up next to the double front door. Rani looked across the gardens to her right. Large cypresses and even taller and broader acers and maples were dotted down the sides of a large expanse of lawn.

'It's not one of those old-world, never-been-touched places, is it, George? I can't stand the cold, or spiders and bugs,' Rani said.

'I think you'll be pleasantly surprised,' he said as he stopped the car. Omar came out of the house to meet them. He was half walking, half running and smiling his broad, welcoming smile.

'I'm pleased you decided to come. The way you ran

out on me last night I thought perhaps I'd scared you off.' Rani felt a pang of desire rise in her chest. Omar led Rani by the hand and almost dragged her through the house at top speed to the terrace at the back.

'You can take the boy off the streets, but... Well, you know the rest. I like a glass of Bucks Fizz with my Sunday lunch,' Omar said, pouring them both a drink. 'Will you join me?' he asked.

Rani accepted. She'd enjoyed the experience the previous night and wanted to repeat it. She took a sip straight away. And felt the tanginess of the orange juice and the fizz from the champagne dance on her tongue. They sat on the terrace and enjoyed the view over the formal gardens while they ate. It was laid out in an Elizabethan style with clipped box hedges and stone paths. As they ate and chatted Rani could feel the knots in her stomach unravelling and when Omar asked her if she'd had any more thoughts on who could be his ghost writer she was ready with her answer.

'What about me?' Rani suggested boldly as if it were the most natural thing in the world. *Oh, my God, he hates the idea*, she thought as he gave away no reaction.

He leant back in his chair, rubbing the stubble on his chin, pondering the proposal. Rani couldn't resist saying something else.

'I've the skills and experience. You've seen my writing. I could have it knocked off in a couple of months. Speedy writing—that's what I'm good at.'

'You've got nerve, I'll say that for you,' Omar finally replied, still looking as if he were weighing up a decision of life and death.

He really hates the idea and now I've gone and made myself look like a fool as well! Rani thought despairingly.

'What about your job at the paper? You'd have to leave it—could you take the risk?' He wanted to test her resolve.

'Don't worry about that. I'll sort something,' she said. 'But I do have a couple of conditions.' Her businesslike manner had returned to her. 'First, it has to pay at least what I earn now.'

'You name your price,' Omar said.

'Second, you must hide nothing from me. If I ask a straight question I expect a straight answer.' Omar approved that with a nod.

'And third,' she said, 'you must pour me another glass of Bucks Fizz.' She knew what she was doing and liked the feeling of letting go. First of all she was throwing in her job and now she was happily getting a little drunk. The recklessness of it all felt liberating and definitely a little dangerous.

'It's a deal,' said Omar, and he obliged her third request immediately.

'To success and to the future,' Omar said, raising his glass in a toast.

'To straight answers,' Rani said shrewdly.

'Right, then, let me show you around,' Omar said. He seemed more at ease than Rani remembered. Perhaps it was the wine or perhaps he was just happier and more relaxed in his own home. He took her by the hand and began to gesture at various items he thought might be of interest.

'That cabinet holds the Lalique,' he said as they breezed through a formal dining room dominated by a long and wide table. 'I'm told the table's made from a single plank of wood, but why that's important I don't know!' They moved into an impressive wood-panelled library, which was filled from floor to ceiling with leather-bound books. Rani tilted her head to read some of the titles. At the door was a shining suit of armour, which looked as if it was fresh out of the packaging.

'It's a fake,' Omar said as he spotted Rani's sceptical gaze. 'It was used in my last film.' There was a collection of swords above an imposing inglenook fireplace and some old portraits in gilt frames, but none of the sitters could possibly be related to her host. As they entered another, smaller room Omar slowed the pace.

'This is my study,' he said. There were various pictures and cuttings taken from newspapers and magazines. He tapped the top of a large wooden filing cabinet.

'Here is all the material you'll need for your research.' His fingers drummed on a pile of papers that obviously couldn't be accommodated inside the cabinet. 'And in here,' he said, tapping the side of his head with his forefinger and smiling.

'Now you know all about me, it's only fair I learn a little bit more about the woman who's going to know me better than any other, don't you think? So tell me, Miss Rani de Silver, who are you?'

Rani was flustered by the question. Usually it was her doing the asking and now the tables were turned she was unsure of what to say.

'Don't be shy,' Omar said. 'I know your name, where you live and what you do for an occupation. I know your age and that you kiss extremely well. So what else will you tell me, or do I have to force it from you?' He pretended to be forceful, which made Rani laugh.

'Well, I love my parents, I pray for world peace every day and I want to work with small children and animals,' she said jokingly. Omar's eyebrows rose an inch higher.

'OK,' Rani said, starting again. 'I dropped out of medical school to become a journalist. I like knowing things you're not supposed to know. I enjoy being with my friends and family on special occasions but I'm not afraid to enjoy my own company. I'm a Leo, my favourite gemstone is sapphire. I like the colour yellow, I don't like pets, but I do like holding hands and kissing in public.' She looked Omar in the eye. 'Will that do?'

'It's enough for now,' he said and again took her by the hand. They chatted away as Omar showed her room after room. Some seemed as if they'd been closed off from the world while others had a friendly, warm feeling with a homely smell. That was certainly true of the kitchen.

'I think this is my favourite room,' Omar said as they entered it. It was large with a long work surface running down one side and a professional-looking range in the middle. There were various appliances dotted along the surface and an eclectic collection of pots and pans.

'I like to cook, and there's no better place to get a really authentic curry than at home, is there? So when I get the chance I come in here and fry up some onions and mix up a keema or a spinach dish.' Rani looked impressed. This was a side to the movie-star playboy she hadn't banked on and it was one that struck a chord with her. She mentally added 'he cooks' to her *For* column.

At the far end of the kitchen was a flight of stairs that took them into a subterranean indoor swimming pool area. There was a sauna and steam room and at the far end a collection of gym equipment.

'Here's another room I like very much,' Omar said, opening a heavy black door. 'It's the cinema. I've been looking at the rushes from the movie in here. Come on in.' For a home cinema it was surprisingly large. There were about thirty seats arranged in tiered rows. It was dark and a film clip was playing. Rani recognised the location as the one she'd been to earlier in the week.

'It's the only chance I get to see the scenes before they're edited,' Omar explained. 'Please forgive me, but I still have a few more minutes to look at. Sit down—you can tell me what you think.' Rani slipped into the seat beside Omar. She was jolted by the electric atmosphere she'd experienced when she'd been close to him before but this was the first time she had really been truly alone with him and she felt safe. The movie flickered in front of them and Rani tried to concentrate on the Omar on the screen rather than being distracted by the one sitting next to her. She enjoyed watching him work, speaking his lines, occasionally fluffing them, laughing sometimes, scowling at the camera and joking. There was a genuine warmth to him when he was unguarded. She could feel herself being turned on. She looked at him and read his eyes. Their alluring brilliance showed he was as excited by her closeness as she was by his. They watched the screen for a few minutes, ignoring the growing feelings they were both experiencing. Rani nervously sipped from the glass she was still holding, aware that her insides were melting.

'Can I top you up?' Omar asked in an effort to defuse the rising tension.

'Yes, please.' Rani gulped. As Omar walked out of the cinema Rani fidgeted in her seat. *What have I got to be afraid of? After all, he's just a man like any other,* she kept telling herself. But that wasn't true and she knew it. He was in a league of his own.

Rani sensed Omar's return. Her body tensed as he sat down beside her again and started the film rolling.

They sat silent and nervous for a few more minutes and then suddenly Rani spoke.

'I need some air,' she blurted, and got up from the chair and almost ran out of the cinema into the kitchen. She lunged at the large French doors that led out to the garden and another patio. Rani blew air from her mouth and fanned her face with her hands at the same time desperately trying to cool herself down before Omar arrived to see what was wrong. Sure enough her host was fast behind her, concern on his face.

'Are you all right, Rani?'

'Yeah, fine!' she lied. The feelings in her stomach and her thighs hadn't quite subsided. 'Just a bit too stuffy in there for me. It's very hot, isn't it? Perhaps it's the champagne!' Rani scrabbled about for a plausible excuse for her actions.

Omar stepped back inside the house and returned within seconds with a glass of cold water.

'Here, have a sip of this. It will make you feel better,' he said, handing the tumbler to Rani. Their hands briefly touched as she took the glass. Rani recoiled slightly, unsure why she had, perhaps afraid of losing the composure she was gradually regaining.

'Come on over here and sit in the shade,' Omar suggested, striding towards a collection of stylish wicker furniture beneath a wide green canvas parasol. Rani took a seat opposite Omar and smiled.

'Are you really sure you want to take on this book?'

'Of course. Why wouldn't I?'

'Oh, I don't know, maybe it's too much, leaving your job and having to come and stay here while it's done. I thought it may be asking too much of you.'

'Not at all,' Rani replied robustly. 'I just have to tell

my editor, that's all. Shouldn't be a problem,' she continued confidently.

'In that case,' Omar said, 'I insist you stay the night.'

Rani looked wide-eyed at him.

'We can go over some of the ideas I've got, stuff I really don't want in it, and then we can head back to town and arrange everything with the publishers. Any chance you could put together something for them by then? I mean, you can use the computer in the office if that would help.'

'Sure, no problem,' Rani replied, hiding her disappointment that he wanted her to stay just so she could work.

Rani looked at the blank screen of the computer. It mirrored her mind. *If in doubt make tea*, she said to herself, and got up from the sumptuous leather chair and made her way out of the office and down to the kitchen. The house was a warren of staircases and rooms. As she walked into the kitchen she was met by Omar. He was wearing an apron with cats on it and had a large knife in his hand. He was expertly chopping onions.

'Nice look,' Rani said, half surprised to see Omar there.

'Thanks. How's it going?' he asked.

'Great!' Rani lied again. 'Really great.' She headed towards the kettle. 'Can I make a cup of tea—er, would you like one too?' she said, realising she wasn't in her own little kitchen in London.

'No, thanks, I'm fine. Help yourself, though. Got everything you need?'

'Yeah, absolutely,' Rani said with convincing fake confidence.

She drummed her fingers on the work surface waiting for the water to boil, hoping that something would come to her, a bolt of inspiration or another major distraction that could fill the void where the writing should be. Nothing happened. Her tea made, she headed back towards the office.

'Don't be long,' Omar called out after her. 'I'm cooking—another half an hour or so.' Rani returned rather woefully to her desk and the waiting computer. The black vertical cursor was flashing at the top of the blank page.

'And you can shut up too,' she said to it.

After a few more minutes of quiet reflection her fingers calmly danced across the keyboard until she stopped to sit back and admire her work.

Silver Screen Dream—the rags to riches story of Omar Khan

'Not bad for two hours' work,' she chided herself. Clearly, sitting down to ghost-write an autobiography was a little more difficult than knocking out a couple of thousand words for her paper.

'Why did I lie and say I'd be able to handle it? I'm out of my depth and I haven't even got into my swimming costume. Aarrgh! And even worse than that, you're talking to yourself again.'

She felt all hot and nervous as she wondered how her father would take the news of her giving up a promising career to write a book—not just that, but a book about an actor, of all trades. It would go down like a bucket of cold sick; she was absolutely convinced.

That night Rani lay in a big guest bed staring up at the ceiling. It felt very strange being alone in such a large room in such a large house while in another room lay the man she felt she was falling so badly for. She had lost track of time but at least the synopsis for the book was written, and Omar's meal had been remarkable. How many women could say Omar Khan had cooked especially for them? It was a consolation of a sort for having a cold bed and a raging conflict of emotions going on inside her head.

Rani tried to visualise the issue. Put simply, she was experiencing feelings she'd not experienced for years. The mix of fear and exhilaration. Like walking a knife edge, on one side overwhelming joy and happiness and on the other utter despair. That was how it had been with David and she was terrified to go there again. He had said he loved her and she'd believed him, believed and fallen for him with every fibre in her body, every drop of blood that coursed round her beating heart. The tall, muscular man who'd wrapped his arms around her and who had promised to shield her from the outside world. Tears began to form in the corners of her eyes and fall silently onto the fresh sheets in which she lay. That man, with a sunshine face and fingers that made her hairs stand on end as they touched her, the man who had professed his love for her and broken her heart.

'What am I doing? What am I doing?' Rani said to herself in a low whisper of a voice. She listened to the night; there was silence within the house and no sense of the wide rolling countryside outside. There was no reply to her call.

CHAPTER FOUR

'THAT SEEMED TO go very well, I thought,' Rani said as they returned to the car.

George had waited for Rani and Omar while they met the publishers; he'd parked on a double-yellow line with the engine running, keeping the limousine warm.

'They seemed to like you,' Omar said, 'and the fact that you seemed to know so much about my films and had recently written an article about me swung it. But now you've signed the contract there's no going back. Whatever I show you or tell you, it's only for the book, agreed?'

Rani smiled at the compliment.

'Agreed. I signed up, didn't I? Well, then, you have my word and my signature.'

The publishers wanted a hit that made a lot of money; Omar didn't care about the money, he was just concerned about getting his version of events out there before his father's. The threat he'd made privately to the publishers that he would not co-operate with the project if Rani wasn't onboard was just a bluff on his part; he knew that. After all, it was he who really wanted to give the world his account of things before his father did. Having Rani write it was just a way of making the process more enjoyable, and so far it had been very enjoyable.

'OK, what next?' he asked when they were sitting comfortably inside the car.

'I'd like you to take me to your home, if that's all right with you. I mean your real home—while we're in a biography kind of mood—where you were brought up. Wouldn't it be a good idea to have a look, see what memories it jogs?'

Omar didn't look at all impressed by the suggestion and Rani could see his reticence; it was written all over his face.

'Go on,' she encouraged him, with soft words and a smile that worked like a charm. 'You know I can only write so many words about what a wonderful cook you are. There really will have to be more to it than a few recipes and your onion-chopping secrets! You never know, you might actually like it!'

Omar seemed unmoved. Rani beamed at him again. This time with the whole of her face. Omar's stubborn scowl began to break, his lips slowly turning upwards to form a smile.

'See, I knew you could do it if you tried hard enough. Now keep practising, a hundred times a day, "I must smile, I must smile".'

'OK, you win,' he said interrupting Rani's chant.

'George, have the rest of the day off. It's time you got home to see that wife of yours. I'll drive.'

George looked stunned.

'Go on, get yourself home,' Omar repeated, and he unlocked the car and got out to open George's door just as the chauffeur always did for him. Then without saying a word Omar took a handful of notes out of his wallet and stuffed them into George's suit pocket, and took the driver's peaked cap from him, sticking it on his own head.

'Bye, George, have a good day,' he said as he pulled away, leaving the abandoned George dumbstruck.

Rani waved out of the back window as the car joined the traffic.

'Will he be all right?' she asked.

'He'll be fine, just have to get used to public transport like everybody else!'

This is going to be an adventure. Forget the day, forget any responsibilities, thought Rani. She was off having fun. Caught up in the excitement of events, she almost forgot that she should have been at work—almost.

'Stop the car,' she bellowed as they passed an old-fashioned red telephone box. Omar stopped the car.

'What's the emergency?'

'I'll only be a moment,' Rani said as she climbed out of the car and headed back to the telephone. Omar watched as she opened the box and began making a call. He couldn't work her out but George was right: she certainly was different from all the others. A few minutes later Rani was back. This time she jumped into the passenger seat next to the multimillion-pound film star.

'Sorted,' she said, a little out of breath.

'What is?'

'Work. I almost forgot, I should be at work really,' Rani said, addressing Omar directly. 'It's OK for you jet-setters to do as you please, but the wage slaves really have other places to be! Anyway, I've told my boss I'm under the weather and wouldn't be in for a day or two.' Rani pointed straight ahead, urging Omar to drive off.

The journey to Manchester was predictably slow along the clogged motorways and A roads but the delays didn't seem to bother either Omar or Rani. They passed the time chatting. Omar discovered that Rani's favourite playback singer was Asha Bhosle. In turn she learnt that Omar had homes in four capital cities and kept the same clothes in every one so he never had to take anything with him when he travelled.

'What about a toothbrush?' she asked jokingly.

'Blue ones in every bathroom.'

'For a boy, eh, and do the ladies all get pink ones when they stay?' she teased.

Omar laughed but didn't answer. It was too close to the bone. Or at least it had been. There was a time when he'd made the most of his fame, but not any longer. The novelty had worn off. He had let too many people into his life who were only after one thing: the chance to let a little of his fame rub off on them. That or to get their hands on his money. It had taken him far too long to realise that the world was full of users and he criticised himself for failing to spot it. After all, hadn't he been brought up by the biggest user of them all, his own father?

'You know, this is the first time I've ever been to Manchester,' Rani offered as they reached the edge of the city. 'Don't look so surprised,' she admonished Omar, who gave her a stare she recognised at once for what it was. 'I've never needed to, have I? But I do know about United, of course, and all those highly paid footballers that are never out of the papers, and I know it's got a great music scene and night life.'

'I wouldn't hold your breath for any of that,' Omar quickly replied. 'That's not the city I came from—that's all a million miles away from where we're heading.'

As she looked out of the window Omar's words seemed far from the reality of what Rani saw. The houses seemed grand and ostentatious. They were set back behind thick, high, well-managed hedges, with expensive cars parked on the drives. The roads were clean and litter free. Chic boutiques sat side by side with upmarket wine bars and restaurants. The people were well-dressed, fashionable, talking into mobile phones and swinging bags emblazoned with the names of designer stores and labels. It didn't look like anything Omar had described—in fact, the exact opposite.

'Should we get out and walk for a bit?' she suggested.

'Sure, why not?' Omar replied as confidently as he could, not wishing to show any hint of the trepidation that he was actually feeling. He pulled into the kerb and stopped the stretched Mercedes outside a clean-fronted sari shop. Large gold letters spelt out the name *Rama.*

Omar got out and opened Rani's door. She was immediately struck by the noise and the smell of the place. Both filled the air. The pungent aromas from the various stalls and shops piled high with industrial quantities of curry and spice mixes burnt their throats as they began walking away from the car. It was exciting and vibrant, full of life. They passed shop after shop selling rolls of brightly coloured fabric. Rani ran her hands across the rainbow of colours, inspecting the quality of the embroidery, just as she had been taught by her mother.

'It's wonderful here, nothing like I'd imagined,' she said, turning to Omar and then moving on, bouncing her hand from roll to roll of fabric until one caught her eye.

'I'll take six yards of this one, please,' she said to a bearded man standing protectively in front of the stall. 'It's for my mum,' she explained, turning back to Omar. Then they began passing the food stalls weighed down with unimaginable mounds of fruit and vegetables, the highly polished red apples and oranges stacked in pyramids. The peppers, garlic and tomatoes offered for sale in wide silver bowls along with bunches of dhaniya. Rani leaned forward to examine the bhindi and deep purple baby brinjal. There were squashes of all colours, bright red chillies and exotic vegetables Rani had never seen before.

She hadn't noticed how far along the road they had come, she had been so absorbed in the immediacy of what she was seeing. Now the noise of the hawkers selling stolen or counterfeit clothing and DVDs rang in their ears like the high-pitched squeal of a pig on the way to the slaughterhouse. The pyramids of fresh fruit had given way to piles of rubbish built up along the pavements, stale rotting food mixed with the discarded packaging from countless cheap-looking food shops and discount stores. The large detached town houses protected from the road with their tall, mature trees gave way to the rows of terraces and overflowing litter bins.

They weaved slowly between the other pedestrians. The affluence of the neighbourhoods diminished with every road junction. Rani suddenly felt the change as if she had stepped from a warm sunny day into the freezing cold heart of winter. It struck her and Omar realised it. They meandered along the streets, into the heart of the neighbourhood, and the precise road on which Omar had grown up. The experience was exhilarating and terrifying for Rani. She had never been anywhere like this before, never seen so many Asian faces in one place. Occasionally she spotted a white one; they stood out like sore thumbs among the men and women wearing traditional Indian and Muslim dress.

'It's just like in the movies,' she said as Omar led her deeper into the sprawling marketplace and deeper into his own past.

'Not the sort of place you're used to, I bet,' he said, 'but it's just like Lahore, and Delhi and Mumbai and all of the other parts of the world where people are scratching a living, and I bet you've never seen them in the flesh either, have you?'

He was right, of course. Rani had never needed to buy her fruit and vegetables from the cheap street sellers, or go to the cloth shops to buy fabric to make her own clothes. She had been born with a silver spoon in her mouth and she could see that stuck in Omar's throat.

'I can't help being born to my parents. It's just the way it is. I didn't choose mine, just like you didn't choose yours, it just happens, so I'm sorry if you feel hard done by or envious of me for that,' she said rather defensively.

'That's a typical answer from someone who's never had to go without, who's never had to fight for what should be theirs,' Omar said bitterly. He was getting angrier the more he saw where he had come from and the obvious distance there was between himself and the world Rani was born into. What he couldn't understand was why that mattered. After all, he wanted for nothing now, did he?

'Two parents, the best of everything, never a thought for what was beyond the fence at the bottom of the pony-club paddock!' He looked around and gestured with his hands. 'All of this a drive away, and you've never even been to see it, and I reckon it wasn't because you weren't curious, you'd be a pretty poor journalist if that was true, but because you didn't even know it was here, did you?'

He was right, of course, and that made the sting of the criticism all the more painful for Rani to take. So she didn't. Instead she turned it back on him and came out fighting.

'Oh, I see what's happening, now you're going to go all working-class hero on me and say how much the streets made you, how the tough life made you the man you are. Well, if that's the case you should be kissing the ground you're walking on!'

As her voice got louder a small number of people stopped to watch the spectacle. 'You don't seem very happy to be back, and why haven't you got a place here rather than that echoing great mansion in the middle of nowhere? Why did you agree to bring me here anyway?'

That told him, Rani thought to herself.

Omar didn't get a chance to reply. Just as he was about to open his mouth a man wearing a leather jacket with the sleeves pushed up and a pair of sunglasses butted in.

'Because he's got a chip on his shoulder, that's why.' The stranger was carrying a roll of brightly coloured orange material. 'In fact you might say he's well balanced…' He paused mid-sentence. Rani shrugged her shoulders as if she was asking why.

'He's got a chip on both shoulders! That's how well balanced he is!' said the stranger, laughing at his own joke.

'Digger? Is that you?' Omar asked with disbelief.

The stranger put down his load and raised his sunglasses.

'The very same. How are you doing, Spud?'

Rani echoed, 'Spud?'

'On account of the chips, of course!' exclaimed Digger.

'And why are you called Digger?' Rani asked.

In an instant Omar's growing temper had subsided. It was as if it had never been there.

'Now I can get my own back,' Omar said as he jumped in before Digger could reply.

'You see, it all started a long time ago, when we used to find bits and pieces of work to make a few quid. Well, Digger here landed up with a job at the council.'

Rani was none the wiser.

'And?'

'He ended up digging graves at the cemetery! And the name just stuck.'

The men gave each other a hug in the middle of the street. Their conversation could have been the reheated leftovers from the day before, they took to each other as if they had never been apart, but it soon became apparent that they'd not seen each other for twenty years. But they picked up from where they'd left off.

'Aren't you going to introduce me to your daughter, then?' Digger prompted and poked Omar. Rani smiled at the compliment, which was as much a backhanded slap for Omar.

'He always was hilarious,' Omar said, patting his long-lost friend on the back. 'Digger, this is Rani, Rani de Silver. Rani meet Digger.'

Digger wiped his hand on his jeans before shaking her hand.

'Pleasure. So what have you been up to since I last saw you?' Digger asked quite innocently of Omar. He caught Rani's eye and winked.

'Moved to Bollywood, become a big film star, made a packet, not much, and you?'

'Pretty much the same story with me actually,' Digger began with a deadpan expression and voice.

'Stopped digging graves, started selling cloth.' He tapped the roll that was now standing on its end.

Rani was wide-eyed at the way they bantered and sparred with one another. Omar had slipped straight back into the streetwise youth he'd been when he'd lived just around the corner from where they were now standing. She could see the root of his quick wit and prickly tongue, clearly sharpened by the verbal exchanges that must have been a constant in his life back then.

'So how's that working out, being an international superstar and playboy? Does it pay well?' Digger asked sarcastically.

Omar moved to give Digger a playful clip round the ear for his cheekiness but Digger was too quick and dodged the hand.

'Still slow, I see,' he said. 'What are you doing back here?' It was the first straightforward, seriously asked question Rani had heard either of them ask. Omar took his time to think about the answer before opening his mouth.

'You know, I'm not really sure,' Omar replied honestly.

Rani helped him.

'I'm actually helping Mr Khan to write his autobiography and I insisted that he take me to the house where it all started. I'm sure you could be an invaluable source of information, Digger,' she said rather awkwardly. 'I mean about his early life, his parents, past *girlfriends*,' she said rather pointedly. 'You know the sort of thing—salacious titbits that sell these kinds of books.'

Digger laughed.

'You want me to dish the dirt on him, is that it? Sure, I can do that, if the price is right.'

'We pay by the anecdote. The more revealing it is,

the better the pay.' Rani enjoyed making Omar squirm as she pushed Digger for something a little juicy. His agitation was showing.

'Well, there was this one time, when we hit on a scheme to make a bit of money on the side, well, it was absolutely foolproof—just a shame we didn't have any fools. It was a disaster.

'Do you remember, Omar? That suitcase full of calculators, they cost us a packet—well, they were pretty expensive things back then. Anyway, we started knocking them out down the market. You remember, don't you, Omar?' Digger kept referring back to his old friend, who didn't seem very amused. Digger pushed on regardless.

'Anyway, they sold like hot cakes. Well, we had 'em so reasonable. Anyway, a bit later one of the punters comes back and says it's bust and wants his money back, then another and then another. Pretty soon we had 'em all back—every one of them was bust. We couldn't make any of 'em work. Could we? Not one!'

Rani encouraged Digger to keep spilling the beans.

'Well, we thought we'd been had and wasted three hundred quid on 'em, all our savings, 'cos we was only boys, remember. Anyhow, a fella comes up to us and says he's interested in 'em. He picks one up and studies it like it's a bit of an antique or something and then proclaims that it's definitely bust but he could use them for spare parts. Well, it was dark and we were cold so we got shot of the lot to him after he offered us twenty-five nicker and even then he says he's doing us a favour. We licked our wounds and think that's that.'

'And?' Rani pressed him.

'We'd been stitched up like a couple of right kippers, hadn't we? The next day he's knocking 'em out left, right and centre. The things were solar powered, weren't they? And there we were selling 'em in the pitch black—no wonder they didn't work!'

'Very good. Have you got a few more like that?' Rani asked.

'Plenty, and then there's the girls—he was always a bit of a ladies' man, even when he was a nipper, was our Omar.'

Omar couldn't restrain himself any more.

'That's great, good to see you, Digger,' he said as he started to steer Rani away. 'We won't keep you any longer—you must be busy,' and he set off along the street.

'Hey, what do you think you're doing?' Rani protested.

'Just looking after you, that's all.'

'Looking after yourself, more like,' she replied. 'I could see you were unhappy with him talking about you like that, but those are just the sorts of things the book's going to need if you want it to sell. You have to give a bit of yourself away, you know, Omar.'

He jostled Rani along the street, as far away from Digger as he could get her before she wriggled free.

'Are you ashamed,' she asked pointedly, 'of where you come from?'

Omar didn't answer but took Rani by the hand and almost dragged her along the pavement. She found it hard to keep up with his pace and thought her hand would come off at the wrist, he was holding onto it so tightly. Omar ducked down back alleys and narrow side roads, negotiating the market stalls and the crowds gathered in search of a bargain. He might not have been back for many years but it was clear he still knew his way around. There was urgency in his movement, like a man who'd been poisoned by a snake and knew he'd only got five minutes to find a doctor with an antidote or the poison would course through his body and consume him. He stopped as suddenly as he had taken off.

'There.' He pointed up, still holding Rani's hand. 'Is that what you wanted to see, the hole I lived in for all those years, the hellhole that was laughingly called home?'

It was like no home Rani had ever seen before. They were standing directly in front of a row of boarded-up decaying shops. Some were still being used. They had paltry-looking stock in the window, old tins of fruit, the labels bleached by the sun. In one there was a lucky-dip barrel with a sign on it, *All tins 10p*. None of them had labels on. The clothes shop next door was shut, steel shutters padlocked to the ground, and daubed with racist graffiti. The next unit was a fish and chip shop. Discarded wrappers and polystyrene boxes littered the pavement outside. The windows were steamed up and the smell coming from the extractor fans was nauseating. The fat in the fryers obviously hadn't been changed for years. But people going in and out didn't seem to notice or care.

'That's where we lived—' Omar pointed firmly to the windows above the shop '—with the smell of the fish and the fat and the stink coming from the streets. Lahore was better than this—cleaner streets, cleaner air and cleaner people.'

Rani looked, open-mouthed. She'd never imagined anyone could exist let alone live behind the brown-stained curtains that hung like rags in the windows. This sort of place had never featured in her life. Why would it? Why would she ever have given it a second thought?

'I'd no idea' was all she could say.

'No, you've no idea. You've got that right,' he said softly. His initial anger had given way to acceptance. Acceptance that life was different for everyone.

'At least you got out,' Rani said, hoping to cheer him up. 'Look at your friend Digger. He's still here and he doesn't seem to be too concerned, so perhaps it wasn't all bad?' she asked, more in hope than with any insight. But she could see something was still eating away at Omar.

'You know, you might be right,' Omar said, turning towards Rani. 'Plenty of people are getting by here.'

'By the look of the place it's a boom town!' she exclaimed rather too enthusiastically. 'Were you ever happy here?'

Omar didn't reply straight away. His eyes darted all along the street and up the buildings, taking in the scene. It was true he had sometimes been happy. He hadn't known any different when he was a boy; it was just the way it was. Him and his dad. They got by. They didn't get along but they got by.

'Perhaps it's not the place,' Omar said quietly, almost to himself.

'I'm sorry, what did you say?' Rani asked.

'Oh, nothing. Nothing here matters any more. Come on, we should get back to the car before we find it up on bricks!'

As they retraced their steps Rani looked constantly around, taking in every sight and smell. It was fantastic atmospheric stuff for the book and it had given her a natural way into it, but at what cost? Omar paced quickly, trying to avoid standing in any of the filth that seemed to cover every square inch of the pavement. He was relieved when they reached the car.

'Seen enough?' Omar asked tightly.

'For the time being,' Rani replied, 'but you never know, I may need to return. I'm sure there are more ghosts like Digger waiting to be sniffed out, aren't there?'

A large sigh was all Omar replied with.

'You may not like it, Omar, but it's just what people want to read about, rags to riches; it offers them hope, doesn't it? If you can make it out of here, then they'll think perhaps there's hope for them too. Don't you see that?'

'I just see squalor and filth.' He turned to look Rani in the face. 'You know, the one thing, the only thing my father ever did for me was to take me away from here, and he didn't do that out of the kindness of his heart.'

'What are you talking about?'

'My dad—' the word almost stuck in his throat '—he took me to Lahore when I was fourteen or fifteen, but it wasn't for the fresh air and a new start. He was running away, running away from this place and the bad debts and the dodgy deals he'd made. We had to leave because there were people out to get him. He was saving his own neck and he took me along because he thought he could sell me in Pakistan. That's the truth of the matter. He wanted to make money from me any way he could. He didn't care what happened to me, so long as he was all right. Well, after he betrayed me once too often I ran off before he had a chance to do it again. Now he's making up for it, isn't he, with his book?'

It was a revelation to Rani and to Omar. He had never let anyone know so much about himself. He'd always kept it tight within his chest. He was breathing heavily. It had been an effort telling her, but he felt better for letting it out. Rani could see the strain on his face. They drove in silence for a few minutes.

'How long has that been eating you up?' she said as gently as she could, putting her right hand up to the side of his face to show him she understood. It was the first time she had made a move to touch him and it seemed like the most natural thing in the world, as if everything was making sense for the first time.

'For twenty years or more.' He smiled and then laughed a little, more out of relief than anything else.

She smiled a caring smile.

'Thank you,' he said as she stroked his face. Rani was looking into his eyes but something behind Omar caught her gaze.

'Stop the car!'

Not knowing what the commotion was, Omar slammed on the brakes and pulled over to the side of the road.

'What is it?' he asked.

'I'm not sure,' Rani replied, and she had opened the door and was off down the road before Omar could question her further. She ran a few yards back along the way they had come. She'd seen something, just a glimpse, but it looked familiar and she needed to take a second look. She stopped outside a large, imposing red-brick building on the opposite side of the busy road. It looked mid-Victorian in age, a deep terracotta-red colour. Beautiful brick construction, if you liked that sort of thing. All the windows had been boarded up and were covered with posters advertising gigs and raves and all sorts of different bands. But it was the carving high up in the wall that she was staring at. She mouthed the letters out as she read them.

'Feed the starving, house the poor.'

There was something very familiar about it but she couldn't put a finger on it even after staring at the letters for a few minutes. She walked back slowly to the warmth of the car pondering the words.

'Are you OK? What was it?' Omar asked.

'I haven't a clue!' Rani replied. 'I thought I saw something—you know how it is, just catches your eye—but I must have been mistaken. It's nothing.'

'You know, you're making a habit of making me stop suddenly,' Omar said.

'I know.' Rani smiled a reply. 'At least it shows you're listening to me, which is a start!' she added cheekily.

'Are you sure?' Omar asked for the third time.

'Positive,' came the firm response.

'OK, then, I will call,' Omar insisted.

'I expect you to.'

Rani watched as Omar drove away. The trip back had been faster than the journey north and falling asleep a few miles out of Manchester had made it pass even faster. She was glad to be back home but unsure if she had made the right decision not to return to Omar's mansion. Her heart was telling her to go and her head was telling her to go but something was holding her back, as it always seemed to do when she felt these deep feelings welling inside herself.

It was no coincidence that she preferred to feel in control of making decisions and situations, asking the questions rather than being asked them. The only time she really let herself go these days was when she was dancing. She could give in to the music without having to worry about the consequences.

Holding onto her emotions was a full-on, twenty-four-seven occupation and meeting Omar in the flesh had seen her drop her guard without really realising it. She'd been bowled over by the encounter, not just the fact that she'd worshipped what she thought he was for so long—after all, she was a mature woman now, wasn't she? Not some silly girl! She could control her feelings and play the game, couldn't she? He'd caught her off guard on the dance floor with a kiss from nowhere, bold, brash—what else would you expect from a man adored by a billion women? He must think he had free rein to do as he wanted! God, how she wanted to let him! But she had to be strong.

'Tea,' she said out loud as she closed the door to her self-contained home. It was a life, but not one she had dreamt of when she was a little girl. Then, it was fields with ponies. Damn it, he was right again! She'd been indoctrinated to find a good man who could provide what her parents had told her were the things every woman needed. But just when she thought she'd found the right man, her prince, it was all taken away from her and she'd retreated into an imaginary shell and constructed a life designed to keep her safe. One that put her in charge, one in which she was in control of the story and especially the writing of the happy-ever-after ending. Being a reporter meant she got to ask the questions. Had Omar believed her when she'd described her article about him as 'journalistic licence'?

The click of the kettle reaching the boil brought Rani's thoughts back to a more practical level. She made her tea and took a comforting sip, which was so hot it almost burnt her lips.

'Right, Omar Khan, who are you really?'

She switched on her laptop and once it glowed with life went straight to Google and searched for pictures of the terracotta building in the heart of Manchester. It only took a few seconds for her to find the images and she began to study them.

Rani zoomed in on the lettering.

'Feed the starving, house the poor.' She repeated the words carved in two-foot-high letters that she'd seen on the building.

She traced her fingers over it. *'Poor,'* she said quietly. It was definitely the building she'd stood in front of a few hours earlier, and then it came to her and she began to feel excited by her detective work. There was a connection with Omar and a small girl in a checked summer dress standing in front of a building, the word 'poor' visible over her shoulder. Omar's mother had been there at some point in her life. Rani clicked on more links and quickly established that it had once been a poorhouse, where the local destitute families of the area could get some form of charity. Opened in 1843, it had taken in orphans, unmarried mothers, the sick and abandoned, until it closed in the 1950s. Her journalist's nose twitched. Why have a photograph taken outside a workhouse? Perhaps because you lived there, or knew it for some reason? Omar's mother must have had connections with the place, so there must be a record somewhere.

Therefore I'll be able to track her down, or perhaps where she came from or went, she thought. Either way Rani was feeling excited with the progress she'd made even though it was too late to make any calls on her theory, but she knew what she'd need to do the following day.

CHAPTER FIVE

THE KNOCK ON the door had a familiar rhythm to it. There was only one set of knuckles in the world that rapped on her door like that and they belonged to her father. Rani gulped. The emotions she'd been suppressing deep inside exploded into her mouth like a bad taste she couldn't get rid of. Her parents had arrived on her doorstep and she knew why. She'd not answered their calls and that was hardly a surprise. After all, she had spent the last seventy-two hours pretending to be ill for her bosses, and being wined, dined and chauffeured by one of the most recognised men on the planet. She'd not been in her flat to take the Sunday-morning call from her mother and she'd still not replaced the broken pieces of her mobile with a new one. She had disappeared from the world and when that happened the alarm bells rang in the mind of a woman like Mrs Anju de Silver.

'Beti, are you in, sweetheart?'

Yes, it was her parents. They had driven the few miles from their very agreeable five-bedroom detached property in Hampstead to their daughter's flat. Rani could hear them discussing her outside the door as she made her way to it.

'I am sure she'll be OK. She is big enough to look after herself now.'

'But this neighbourhood, it's so rough, anything could have happened to her.'

'It's Battersea, not the Bronx!'

'She could be lying in a pool of blood for all you know. She's my daughter,' said Mrs de Silver. Her husband didn't bother to point out the obvious and allowed his wife to let her imagination run away with her. Rani cagily opened the door.

'Abu ji, Mumma, what a lovely surprise.' Rani could act; she hadn't spent all those years in the school drama club for nothing.

'Come on in. What brings you all the way over here?' She carried on the pretence as best she could as she stepped aside and let her parents in. Rani watched as their hawkish eyes went to work scanning the flat for signs, for clues as to what had been going on.

'We hadn't heard from you, darling, that's all, and we were passing on our way down to your Uncle Sanjay's so we thought why not pop in to see if you were all right,' Rani's mother said unconvincingly.

'Just passing, eh?' repeated Rani. 'But you've time for some chai, surely, Mummy,' and she turned to her father, whom she could always persuade of her innocence. 'Daddy ji, tea?' she asked.

Her parents looked at each other. Neither had been able to spot anything out of place or amiss.

'That would be lovely, Rani, if it's not too much trouble,' her father said.

'Of course not. There's nothing like tea, is there?' Rani's enthusiasm was her undoing. It was a telltale trait that had always pointed to her hiding something and her parents were well aware of it.

'You've been busy?' her mother asked with all the skill of a Venus fly trap waiting to snap shut on some unfortunate bug. Rani spotted the ambush and side-stepped it.

'You know, much the same as ever. Always busy in my line of work, Mummy. How are you two?' she added, hoping to deflect any more probing.

'Both very well, thank you, Rani. Would you expect anything different?' her mother replied, not being the sort of woman put off that easily.

'No, not at all.' Rani began to stutter, another indication to her parents that she was not being completely straight with them. While her mother continued to prod at her with the precision that years of dealing with other consultants and their fussy, busybody wives let you develop, Rani's father spotted the flashing lights on the answer phone.

'You've been away?' He tossed the question in among all of his wife's and Rani instinctively answered 'no'.

'So you got all my messages, then? But just didn't bother answering them.' The trap snapped shut and Rani realised she'd been caught out by better players of the deception game than herself.

'Not so much away, but out. I've been on assignment. I mentioned I've been busy, didn't I?'

'We've seen your article.' The words landed deep in Rani's heart the moment they left her father's mouth.

'Oh!' was all she could manage to say.

'Oh—is that the best you can do for a response? You, *"the woman who went face to face with the Lion of Bollywood and found out he was a pussy cat"*.'

Rani winced as her father recited the quote that had been used to caption her photograph in the paper beside the interview with Omar Khan.

'So you've read it, then?' Rani said rather sheepishly.

'Yes, we've read it, after everyone at the hospital and

the clinic rubbed it in our faces, yes, we've read it.' The obvious anger and disappointment was notable in every word her father spoke. 'What sort of nonsense is this? Is this what you gave up studying to be a doctor for, so you could write drivel like this about men like that?'

Rani felt ashamed. For all the years she had lived alone and supported herself, she could be brought back to earth with a bump and made to feel like an eleven-year-old again in an instant. Such was the hold her parents still had on her. She consoled herself that they had no idea what she'd been up to over the past three days. Spending a night with a film star, no matter how innocent it was—if they knew that, oh, my God, Rani thought, the pair of them would probably explode on the spot!

'We called your office and they said you'd been off ill since you'd done the interview. Are you OK now, dear?' her mother asked with a more conciliatory approach than her father.

'Yes, much better, thanks, Mum. I'll make that tea,' Rani said, taking the opportunity to leave the room and gather her thoughts. What else did they know? Rani couldn't be sure, but found herself weighing up all the possibilities and conceiving of some ideas they might have that hadn't occurred to her before. And then, after taking a couple of deep breaths, she said to herself, *Rani, you're a grown woman, behave like one! Front them out!* She returned to the living room with a tray of tea and cups and some small Danish shortbreads that she thought might ease her father's mood. *I'll let them make the first move.*

An air of false civility fell upon them as Rani poured cups of tea and handed them to her parents.

'So just passing, eh?' She threw caution to the wind

and decided to go on the attack and see where that got her.

'We were worried. That's what parents do—worry about their children,' her mother said acerbically.

'And with good reason, by the looks of things!' her father chipped in.

'What's that supposed to mean?' Rani knew very well what her father was thinking but she wanted to make him say it for himself rather than spoon-feed him or take the criticism lying down.

'You know very well, Rani. Running around with these types, heaven knows where it could end—they're only after one thing.'

That made him blush and Rani smile. Her father would never use the *s-e-x* word unless he was describing a medical condition.

'I'm just glad we got here when we did and nipped any nonsense in the bud. I'm not having my daughter cavorting with a man like that.'

Now Rani blushed from the inside out. She could feel the guilt rising through her body, spreading from her stomach along her arms and legs. Her fingers and even her ears seemed to be red-hot with embarrassment.

'Well, you've nothing to fear on that score.' She pushed on with her aggressive denial of events, both to her parents and to herself. After all, it was true—she hadn't slept with him, had she? She'd thought about it, thought about giving herself completely, and was being torn apart by the conflict going on in her mind and heart—not wanting to be hurt so badly again, but not wanting to die a spinster either! The choice was unenviable.

Her parents finished their tea, but, instead of looking as if they were ready to go, they looked as if they'd taken root.

'Don't let me keep you. I know you've got to get going to Uncle Sanjay's, haven't you? Send him my love and Aunty.' Rani stood up and collected her mother's handbag and her father's jacket.

'It was a lovely surprise, the pair of you popping over like that, most spur of the moment for you, but I've got to get on so…'

'We know when we're in the way,' her mother said with a sniff.

'Mummy, it's not like that at all, but I've still got a bit of a cold—' she forced a cough to underline the point '—and I don't want you catching it and I've got work to be getting on with, so if you don't mind…'

Reluctantly her parents took the hints and gathered their belongings.

'Just so long as you're OK,' her mother said.

'Yes, I'm fine, Mum, honestly.'

'Just so long as you're not pregnant,' her dad added.

'Daddy!'

As she closed the door on her parents Rani slid to the carpet with her head in her hands.

'Oh, my God, what am I thinking? I can't go through all of that again, not that agony,' she said to herself. 'But I want to be with him, I really want to be with him!' *In for a penny, in for a pound*, she thought, and immediately dialled her boss, Tony. While she waited for him to answer she began rehearsing what she was going to say. In the end it wasn't half as bad as she'd imagined.

'Hello, Tony, it's Rani. Have you got five minutes?'

'For my star interviewer, of course, fire away.'

The build-up made it even worse but Rani pressed on.

'Funny you should mention interviewing, because it's about the Omar Khan interview that I'm calling.'

'Go on.'

'Well, he's—you're not going to believe this, but—he's asked me to ghost-write his autobiography for him.' And then she garbled out the last few words, 'But the publishers want it like yesterday, and I need to quit work to do it, so please don't shout but I need to resign!'

There were a few seconds of silence while Tony untangled exactly what had been said.

'I see,' he replied, and then paused again. 'You want to quit your job, eh? How long do you reckon this tome will take to write?'

'About three months if I do it full time.'

'Why don't you ask me for a career break instead of quitting?' he suggested.

'You'd do that for me?' Rani exclaimed as the consequences of his offer sank in.

'Sure, why not? It will give us a chance to try out some new writers. Go on, I'll give you three months starting from tomorrow. Deal?'

'Yes, of course, that's great, you're great, that's really fantastic, you're really fantastic, Tony, thank you, thank you, thank you.'

'Happy, then!'

Rani blew a great big kiss down the phone.

'I'll get HR to send over some paperwork, just sign it and send it back, and make sure you've got a new phone by the time you come back!'

'I will, I promise. I'll get two! Thanks, Tony.'

Full of excitement, Rani walked around the flat flitting from one thing to another. She tidied the teacups, rearranged her DVDs, stacked a pile of papers on her desk, put the kettle on, loaded the washing machine and was about to start dusting when the doorbell rang.

'I've brought some wine,' Shilpa announced.

'And I've ordered pizza,' Sunita added, 'so you're in for a long night of cross-examination,' she said as Rani opened the door.

'Hello, stranger, he let you go, then? I had visions of you manacled to a bed—you weren't, were you?' Shilpa asked as she made herself at home.

'Don't be daft.' Rani dismissed such an outrageous suggestion but suddenly couldn't help but think about being in such a position. She was finding it hard to concentrate, to prevent her mind from flitting back to the moment in Omar's Mercedes when she had stroked his face and felt overcome by such a powerful feeling.

'But you've been away for days so something must have happened. Go on, you can tell us, we won't tell a soul,' said Sunita. 'Will we?' she said, looking at Shilpa, who shook her head and pursed her lips.

'All your sexy secrets are safe with us,' Shilpa assured her.

'Oh, the pair of you, you're impossible!' Rani exclaimed.

'So it's true, then—there are some sexy little secrets? Great, fetch some glasses. This is going to be an enormous evening!' Shilpa said as she unscrewed the top of the bottle she was carrying.

'Maybe I've nothing to say,' said Rani innocently with a hint of playfulness.

'Yeah and pigs have got wings, right! Come on, spill the beans and don't leave out any of the juicy bits because we'll know you're lying,' Sunita replied.

Rani broke into a broad grin.

'I knew it, I knew it!' Shilpa said, dancing up and down and pointing a finger at Rani. 'You little minx.'

Rani's grin stretched across her entire face as she battled to contain it. She'd been dying to let someone know about her date with Omar.

'OK, OK, so I stayed at his place. Where's the harm in it?' she teased them.

'And where is it? What's it like?' asked Sunita.

'Did he have black satin sheets and a mirror over the bed?'

'Shilpa!' Rani reacted. 'It wasn't like that. Ooh, you're impossible! Pass me a glass of that wine, will you? I'm going to need it if I'm going to tell you just what went on.'

The friends snuggled down on the sofa, Shilpa sitting up on a pile of cushions on the floor facing Rani, who was happy to let them into some of the detail about her time away. The pizzas arrived and another bottle of wine was opened as Rani described the house with its luxurious indoor pool area and Omar's cooking ability.

'So he can cook! Big whoop—but you're not after his skills in the kitchen, are you? It's his skills in the bedroom that are important!' Shilpa thundered, disappointed that her friend actually hadn't managed to throw herself into the arms of the Lion of Bollywood.

'Did you even get to see his bedroom?' she asked hopefully.

Rani smirked.

'No, I didn't!' she protested, thinking back at just how close she had been to giving into him and her own feelings while they had sat in his private cinema. What was it that had stopped her? she wondered. She had hoped she'd be able to put it down to her sense of self-worth but *this was* Omar Khan, the man of her dreams and her bedroom wall. She was not going to let a little thing like propriety get in the way of such a moment. She was a twenty-first-century woman—she wasn't going to be dissuaded by how guilty she felt towards her parents, was she? No, the reason she hadn't caved in to her own burning feelings was even more powerful than the respect she had for her mother and father. Quite simply she didn't want to feel the pain again, the pain of loving and the pain of losing, a hurt so strong it made you cry with happiness and want to run and never stop running to escape the heartbreak.

'So you're going to see him again, I hope.' Sunita's question brought Rani back to her own living room from the depths of her soul. She was startled by the sound and had to ask Sunita to repeat it.

'Sorry, what?'

'I said will you be seeing him again? I guess you were away somewhere in a fantasy, weren't you, dolly day dream?'

'Oh, um, yes, something like that. Well, yes, actually, I will be seeing more of him—quite a bit more actually,' Rani replied, still only half conscious of what she'd been asked.

'See, told you so, and I bet I can tell you which bits she'll be seeing most of!' Shilpa laughed at her own joke.

'Shilpa,' Rani chastised her friend. 'It's really not like that.'

'Not yet it's not! Just you wait, the moment you drop your guard, or anything else for that matter!

They all started laughing at Shilpa's analysis of the situation.

'Actually…' Rani began.

Her friends sat bolt upright.

'Actually,' Rani continued, 'he's asked me to ghost-write his autobiography. Remember I told you in the club that he was looking for a writer? Well, I've persuaded him to let me do it.'

'And just where were you when he agreed to that?' Shilpa asked.

'No, we weren't in bed,' Rani exclaimed, knowing just how Shilpa's mind worked.

'What do your mum and dad think about that?'

Rani suddenly became all serious with the mere mention of her parents.

'I've not told them. They were here this morning actually, checking up on me, just like you two. Is there no one who thinks I'm old enough to make my own decisions and live my own life?'

'Nope,' Sunita and Shilpa said in unison.

'And I'm making a wild stab in the dark here, but I guess if you've not told them about the book thing, you've certainly not told them about how you feel about Omar, have you?' Sunita asked.

Rani shook her head.

'I've only kissed him once, and although it was very enjoyable, even if I didn't tell him, it's hardly grounds for marriage.'

'Marriage, exactly, that's what your mum will be plotting and I hate to think about how your father feels. I mean, this man isn't even a dentist,' Shilpa pointed out.

'Shilpa!'

'Well, you know what Rani's mum's like. She'll know, mark my words. She's got that kind of insight, hasn't she? She's just not told Rani she knows because then she can hold it in reserve—you know, she'll blackmail you with it or something,' offered Shilpa by way of explanation.

'That's a bit harsh, don't you think?' said Sunita.

'You've met her mum!' exclaimed Shilpa.

'Fair point.'

Rani tried to look affronted but she knew her two best friends were probably right. Mothers always knew their children and Asian mothers made it their business to know their children better than most.

'So how are you going to cram writing this book into your already busy and increasingly complicated life, then?' Sunita asked.

'I'm taking a break from work.'

'Giving up?'

'No, not that bad—at least that's a good thing, isn't it? I mean, when I do tell Mum and Dad, that's in my favour, isn't it?' Rani was clutching at straws like the drowning woman she was, drowning in the mire of her own making.

'Yeah, I'm sure they'll be fine with that.' Sunita tried to offer some reassurance, which was immediately undermined by Shilpa.

'It's him abandoning you with unborn twins that they'll have difficulty with.'

'Oh, Shilpa, do shut up!'

They fell about laughing again. The wine and the good company made for an enjoyable evening.

'You do realise that every woman in the world would kill to be in your shoes right now,' Sunita said, addressing Rani, who was by now lying stretched out on one of the sofas.

'You mean drunk on a couch with a coffee table covered in cold pizza?' Shilpa suggested.

'Stupid!' exclaimed Sunita. 'You know very well what I meant—close to a Bollywood hunk who seems to have the hots for you and who's now asking you to move in with him in the interests of *research.*' She emphasised the last word by making quote marks with her fingers.

'So what are you driving at exactly?' Shilpa asked, her mouth forming the words with utmost precision due to the wine she had been drinking. Rani was almost oblivious to the fact she was being discussed.

'I mean, Shilpa,' Sunita said, the wine also making her speak quite deliberately to make sure she was understood, 'I mean, what is really holding Rani back from becoming Omar's leading lady, if you get what I'm saying?'

'Simple,' proclaimed Shilpa. 'Age. She doesn't want to be pushing him around in a wheelchair when he's an old man and mushing up his food for him. Age! That's your answer!'

Rani realised her best friends were now staring at her with the quizzical faces of people who were a little drunk and thought they were discussing the meaning of life or a similarly important subject. She scanned their swaying heads for a moment, one to the other and back again. And sighed.

CHAPTER SIX

RANI WOKE UP feeling a little woozy from the previous night's wine but still floating on a cloud of dreams. She was taking positive control of her destiny and making grown-up decisions. She was proud of herself and hoped her confidence would rub off on her parents. She didn't have long to test the theory. The phone rang and without thinking Rani picked it up.

'Hello, Rani de Silver,' she answered automatically.

'I'm very well aware of who you are,' the voice on the other end of the line began in an urgent angry tone. 'The question is do you know who you are?'

'Daddy ji?'

'That's right! It's your father,' Dr de Silver bellowed down the phone. 'What have you got to say for yourself?'

Rani was at a confused loss of what to say since she had no idea what her father was going on about. She could hear the raised voice of her mother on the line as well, trying to control her husband.

'Hello, darling.' Her mother had obviously wrestled the phone from her husband's grip. 'Are you OK, my lovely?'

Rani blinked her eyes into focus and shook her head to wake herself up enough to concentrate.

'I believe so, Mummy. I only saw you yesterday. What's the matter?'

There was a moment's hesitation in her mother's voice before she continued.

'Have you seen the papers this morning?'

Rani was having trouble seeing anything too clearly and she certainly hadn't seen the papers.

'No, why?'

'Because you're all over them! That's why!' her father exclaimed. He'd obviously grabbed the phone back. 'Even in our paper!'

Rani wondered what could have happened, why she would be in the papers, what reason? Her mind fell into gear. It must have something to do with Omar; it must.

'And you said you had only interviewed the man.'

Rani's heart sank. What were her parents looking at? she wondered. She didn't need to wait as her father began to quote from his paper.

'"Who is the mystery woman seen arm in arm with Bollywood legend Omar Khan? The glamorous brunette was caught cavorting with the film hunk as he paid a surprise visit to Manchester recently. Whoever she is she certainly seemed captivated by the star and he seemed spellbound by her charms too!"'

'Well, what is the meaning of all this, eh?' Dr de Silver asked brusquely.

'Oh, that,' Rani said as lightly as possible. 'Oh, it's nothing, nothing at all. I was with him. Yes, that's right, I remember.'

'Huh, you remember now, eh! But not when you're talking to your parents just yesterday. What's wrong with you? Your memory going now you've hit twenty-five, is that it?'

'Calm down, Pappa,' his wife urged. 'Are you OK, Rani, really?' she asked with more concern.

'Yes, I'm fine, Mummy, honestly.'

'Honestly? You don't seem to know the meaning of the word!' Her father's voice was still dominating the three-way conversation.

'Well, stay where you are. Daddy and I are on our way over to you right away.'

The phone went dead. Clearly her parents were heading towards her and with the speed and force of a cannonball by what Rani could make out. She darted into the kitchen, filled the kettle and prepared a cup of tea. She turned on the shower and while it was warming gathered the evidence of the girls' night in and plumped the cushions. With a mug of tea in her hand she stood in the shower, hoping that it would revive her and give her the power to think through what was happening. Someone had obviously taken a picture of Omar and her when they were out and given it—or sold it, more like—to the papers. She racked her brain to think of who could have done it and came up with just two possible names: Omar, or the man they'd met—Digger.

While the water cascaded down her body Rani weighed up the motive that each suspect might possibly have. The finger of suspicion pointed squarely at Digger. *OK, what to do now?* Rani pondered, knowing it would only take her parents about forty minutes to land on her doorstep. She had to be ready to defend herself. *I'll own up to writing the book*, she thought. *I'll even tell them about the career break, paying special attention to the fact that it's just a break, I've not given up or anything like that. The rest we'll play by ear!*

Rani stepped out of the shower much more relaxed than she had stepped in. She had a battle plan and being prepared when talking to her parents was always an advantage. She carefully selected what to wear, a modest blouse and cardigan that her mother had bought for her, but she hardly ever wore, and sensible trousers and shoes. She checked the supply of Danish shortbread, refilled the kettle and then gave the living room a quick vacuum.

'Oi, what's all the noise for?' Shilpa said, trying to be heard above the sound of the vacuum cleaner. Rani jumped with surprise.

'Aaah, what are you doing here?' she said, eying her friend up and down. Shilpa was wearing one of her old nighties and was suffering from the worse case of bed head Rani had ever seen.

'We stayed, remember,' Shilpa shouted. 'Can you turn that off? I've a banging headache as it is.'

Rani flicked the switch but continued to straighten the room and put the leftover pizza into the bin.

'Oh, that's better,' Shilpa said, clutching her forehead. 'Now I just need water, paracetamol and another five hours in bed and I'll be as right as rain.'

'Oh, God, I forgot you two were here,' Rani exclaimed.

'What's up?' Sunita enquired as she emerged from the bedroom.

'My parents, that's what. They've found out about me and Omar. It's all in the papers.' Rani looked at her friends. 'It wasn't either of you, was it?'

'What wasn't us?' Sunita asked, looking terribly confused and in as bad a state as Shilpa.

'No, never mind, it can't have been,' Rani said almost to herself. 'Worse still, Mum and Dad are on their way over and they'll be here at any time. You've got to get out.'

But there wasn't time. The familiar knock on the door signalled the arrival of Rani's parents.

'Quick, back in the bedroom!' Rani urged her two friends to retreat. They moved swiftly, Shilpa grabbing a glass of water on the way.

'Rani, are you there?' her father called out.

'Coming,' she said as confidently as possible as she made her way to the door. 'This is a nice surprise—two visits in as many days.'

'Are you on your own, dear?' her mother asked. 'It's just that we thought we could hear voices.'

'Quite alone,' Rani replied as she glanced quickly back to the closing door of the spare bedroom. She gave her mother a kiss on both cheeks and then her father, who was carrying what looked like a pile of newspapers in his hands.

'I'll get straight to the point,' he said as he was still walking towards the sofa, and he put a copy of the paper under Rani's nose. 'Here's the picture I was telling you about, you and that roughneck.'

Rani took the paper from her father and sat down with it. The image was clear and showed Omar and herself arm in arm walking along the street. The headline posed the question: Who's that girl?

'So what have you got to say for yourself?' her father began.

'I say let's have some tea!'

'You stay there and answer your father,' Rani's mother said firmly. 'I'll make the tea.'

'So what's it all about, Rani?'

'I can see how it all looks,' Rani began, 'but it's all quite innocent. But before I go any further I think you should sit down.'

'Oh, my God, you are pregnant!' her father proclaimed in a doom-laden voice.

'Oh, Daddy, it's not like that. Mr Khan has been asked to write his autobiography.'

'Write? I bet he can't write. I bet he signs his name with an X,' Dr de Silver butted in.

Rani did her best to ignore the slur and remain in control of her feelings and the tone of her voice, although faced with such provocation it was hard.

'As it happens, he liked what I had written about him following the interview and he kindly asked me if I would help him. And before you say anything more, Daddy, I accepted his offer. I've already met the publishers and they liked my proposal.' Rani felt confident in her self-assured approach.

With their ears to the door, Sunita and Shilpa were enjoying the overheard conversation.

'Go, girl, you tell them!' Shilpa whispered to Sunita with a smile. Her friend motioned her to be quiet.

'What was that?' Rani's mother said as she sat down with a tray of tea. 'I thought I heard something.'

'Just the window in the spare bedroom, Mum. I've got it open—probably just blown something over,' Rani improvised quickly. She began to pour the tea and hand it out to her parents.

'So you're writing a book now.' Mrs de Silver started the conversation back up again. She wasn't going to be sidetracked from discovering the truth by an open window.

'Yes, that's right, I was just telling Dad. It's a fantastic opportunity—' But she didn't get a chance to finish her sentence before her mother jumped in.

'Rani, we know you, I gave birth to you, so please

tell us what this is all about and none of your storytelling, please.' Her mother was direct and to the point.

'As I say, it's a great opportunity. I've always wanted to do something like this,' Rani soldiered on, not wanting to be pushed off course by her mother's interruption.

'And how are you going to fit in all this writing with work, and what were you doing being photographed in the street with this man, and what on earth were you doing in Manchester in the first place?'

'You know what the press are like, Mummy ji. It only takes someone with a camera to take a picture and sell it and this is what you end up with. Anyone can do it these days—just point your mobile phone and send it off to the papers. Anyway, it's all been taken out of context. Look—' and she pointed at the picture '—after we'd met the publishers I asked Mr Khan if we could go to Manchester to see where he'd been born and raised.'

'So you ended up tramping up and down in the gutter!' her father chipped in.

Rani ignored him and carried on.

'So that's why we went and, as you can see, he's holding me up. In fact he actually caught me as I stumbled, that's why he's got his arm in mine, and I'm looking up at him like that because I was obviously tripping. You see, it's all very innocent if put back into context.'

'I see,' said Mrs de Silver, 'but what about work?'

'I was coming to that.' Rani boldly marched on. 'I've arranged a career break for three months, to give myself the time to write. They're keeping my job open for me, so I go back when it's done.' She felt triumphant, like an Olympian who had just won a gold medal, or a mountaineer who had just made it to the summit of Everest. As far as she was concerned she had put up an excellent defence to her parents' repeated assault on her position.

'And what about your pension, eh?'

Rani knew her father would ask about that, it was just the sort of question he would put to her, and she was ready with a complete answer.

'Everything is safe. I return to work on exactly the same terms as I left. My pension is safe—of course, I won't pay into it for three months, that's true, but, Daddy, you know far better than me about the vagaries of the Stock Market, and what is lost in one year can be made up in a single day, isn't that true?' She knew she was right to flatter his ego. He nodded sagely. 'And anyway, I have the ability to pay in extra contributions, so I can always make up that small amount if need be. You see, Daddy, I have thought it through and see it as a business opportunity, to forge another career, just like you did when you went into private practice.' *Flattery and fathers go hand in hand*, Rani thought to herself. He changed his tack.

'You know we don't approve. How could we?' His tone softened. 'But we're your parents and we care. whatever you might be thinking now, we care about what happens to you and we don't want you to be hurt.'

'Don't want me to be happy, more like,' Rani retorted.

'No, it's not like that, Rani. Your father doesn't mean it like that. He's very concerned about you, just like I am, and we don't want to see you taken in by this showman.'

'Huh, what's there to be taken in by? And anyway, it's not as if we are actually an item, is it?' Rani snorted. She was actually thinking to herself just how taken in she had been by him, not the outward signs he gave away to the public for free, but the private side only she had seen of him in Manchester and the man cooking for her in his palatial kitchen. She continued to stand her ground and, no matter how her parents phrased their questions about the true nature of her relationship with Omar, Rani didn't back down. After all, they weren't an item; she didn't have a relationship with him in the way they kept intimating; it was purely professional. Dr and Mrs de Silver hadn't really encountered such a display from their only child before and it took them a little by surprise. But Rani was sticking to her guns and wouldn't be distracted.

'So that's your final decision, is it? Throw away a promising career and take up with a movie star!'

Rani put her head in her hands. After half an hour of heated discussion her father had moved not one step closer to compromising his views. She might as well have been talking to the teapot! she thought to herself.

Collecting their coats, Rani's parents headed out of the flat, fazed by her unwillingness to be won round to their point of view. The last time she had appeared so headstrong was when she dropped out of medical school.

'We'll be off, then,' her mother said rather haughtily. 'But don't forget, you know where we are. It's still your home, beti, you know that.'

A last little swipe and a dollop of guilt for good measure, Rani thought as she closed the door on them. She stood there for a moment listening to them still deep in animated conversation.

'She gets that from your side of the family—you know that, don't you?' her father said.

'My side!' exclaimed her mother.

'Yes! Your side. She's just like you and your own

mother and, as far as I can remember, your grandmother as well!'

'Too soft, that's the problem, you should have been tougher on her...'

Their words faded but the argument about their daughter's genetic inheritance very likely continued all the way down in the lift and all the way back home.

The door to the spare bedroom swung open and Shilpa and Sunita fell out and over each other in a desperate race to the bathroom.

'I thought they'd never leave!' Shilpa said, barging ahead of Sunita and closing the door.

'Shilpa! Hurry up. I'm bursting out here!' she pleaded.

'So you don't want any tea, then?' Rani joked.

'Oh, Rani!'

Shilpa emerged from the bathroom, her face showing the evident relief.

'That seemed to go pretty well,' she said. 'From where we were, of course,' she added. 'I've not seen your mum and dad lost for something to say before. A very strange occasion, that's for sure. What are you going to do now?'

Rani thought for a moment and then said triumphantly, 'I'm going to buy a new phone and then pack! I've got a book to write!'

'And a hunk to hook!' Shilpa added, unable to help herself.

CHAPTER SEVEN

'I'VE MADE UP the guest suite for you, Miss Rani,' George said as he led her up the grand staircase to the second floor of the house. 'There are wonderful views from there of the park at the back of the house and it's not too far from the office. Mr Khan said that you'd be needing to work in there—is that right?'

'Well, I've brought my laptop so I can write anywhere, but I suppose I'll need to rummage through all the cuttings. Thank you, George, and please do call me Rani.'

'As you wish, Miss Rani,' he said, opening the door to the suite.

'Talking of Mr Khan, where is he?'

George placed Rani's cases on top of the bed, while she put the two make-up boxes and the laptop onto the dressing table.

'He's at the set today, miss, wanted to drive himself, he said, and anyway, after you'd called someone needed to be here to collect you from the station. Will that be all?'

Rani began to smile and covered her mouth.

'Oh, George, you sound like one of those old butler characters from the Victorian Age! No, I'm fine, thank you, just fine. You'll be bowing next and walking out of the room backwards!'

They smiled at each other and then Rani was alone. She had an urge to explore the house, to rifle through all the drawers and bedside cabinets, not looking for anything in particular but just out of a sense of curiosity, out of sheer nosiness. But she restrained herself, instead taking the time to unpack her clothes. After all, she was going to be there for a while and that required making the place feel like home. Carefully she arranged her underwear and night clothes into one of the drawers. She hung up a range of dresses in the wardrobe. Before she placed each one in, she held it against her slim frame and paraded in front of the full-length mirror to remind herself just how much she liked each item. Then she put matching shoes beneath each accompanying outfit.

Looks like I'm moving in! she said to herself as she placed everything. She took her toothbrush and shampoo and put them in the massive bathroom and began fiddling with the taps, trying to get them to work. She gave up and returned to the bedroom. It was a curious sensation, feeling like a guest with the run of the place, but also feeling like a charlatan because she had no real idea if she could actually write a book, and in some ways she knew she had only accepted the opportunity because she wanted to be closer to Omar.

'I must have some sort of self-destructive death wish going on,' Rani said out loud. After all her feelings were pulling her in three hundred and sixty directions at once. Agreeing to live in his house for three months was just a ludicrous thing to do if she was trying to prevent herself from driving down the David cul-de-sac again.

Utter, utter madness, she thought, jumping on the giant bed and lying down when she'd finished unpacking. But however mad Rani felt she was being, she couldn't help but giggle out loud at the newness and excitement of it all. *Right then, Mr Omar Khan, let's see what we shall see*, and she pushed herself up from the bed and slipped out of her room and headed along the landing. She knew she must look ridiculous tiptoeing along the corridor trying not to disturb anything or make a sound. From the walls an eclectic collection of paintings were hung. Rani was no expert but some looked very much like pictures she'd seen by Picasso and Warhol.

Were they for show or there because he actually liked them? she mused. If they were genuine they certainly cost a lot of money, that was for sure. She passed two more guest rooms and a large landing, like an open-plan reading room of a dusty museum or library. It bowed out in a pear shape and was surrounded by giant windows, which gave a one-hundred-and-eighty-degree view of the countryside. She crept slowly past the windows until she instinctively stopped outside another door. She knew it must be Omar's room. It felt as if it should be.

I wonder if Shilpa's right—have you got a mirror over the bed? She tried to convince herself that she was too well brought up to go around sneaking into people's bedrooms, that it was definitely the wrong thing to do, but she had an overwhelming desire to see if Omar had satin sheets and other displays of a playboy lifestyle, something tacky that would demonstrate just how unsuitable he was for her. Rani hovered on the threshold, her hand on the doorknob, her good angel and bad devil once again dancing on her shoulders.

'In for a penny, in for a pound,' she murmured to herself and gently eased the door open. What confronted her almost took her breath away. Where she expected to see a giant bed with surround-sound plasma screens was a simple mattress in the middle of the room. It was unpretentious, covered in white linen and a simple throw. There were no chrome chairs or stainless-steel futuristic furniture, just a plain wooden table with a small mirror and a few bottles of aftershave. There was no minibar or frivolous extravagances; on the walls were pictures of rural views, perhaps of India or Pakistan. In the bay window area she recognised a daybed, the sort of thing her aunty in Mumbai used to rest on. She stood staring out of the window lost in her own thoughts and didn't have any idea that George had been standing behind her. He gave a gentle little excuse-me cough to announce his presence. Rani flinched.

'I didn't mean to startle you,' he apologised.

'Sorry, pardon, George? I think I was a million miles away.'

'I said, I didn't mean to disturb you. I just wondered if there was anything I could do for you, miss.'

It was then Rani realised where she was and suddenly she became instantly overcome with embarrassment about the situation and what George must think of her. He didn't say a word while Rani thought quickly.

'Actually, there is, George. I'd love a bath, but I couldn't make the taps work. It's like being in a hotel and feeling silly asking.'

'Not at all, miss.' And he led the way back to the guest room and demonstrated how the taps worked. 'If that is everything I'll be getting along,' George said, and left without mentioning his discovery of Rani in Omar's room. She breathed a huge sigh of relief that the awkwardness was over. *But what if he tells Omar? Oh, God, what will he think of me? Perhaps George won't say anything.* The thoughts and scenarios played out quickly in her mind as she waited for the bath to fill. Rani was struck by the outward opulence of the house; the bathroom she was sitting in, for example—it was bigger than the whole of her flat and clearly made of very expensive marble. She remembered how Omar had shown off the various priceless collections with an almost disdainful dismissive wave of his hands as she had been shown around. And then there was Omar's room. It was a complete contrast to everything else. Plain and simple, almost humble, a world away from everything that surrounded it, a core of ordinariness, enrobed in opulence. *Why?*

The hot water made Rani drowsy. But it was a price worth paying for enjoying such a warm and luxurious bath. She stretched out full length and even found there was space to roll over and over. It was a wonderful feeling, liberating to be naked in so much water. She had always wanted to swim without any clothes or inhibitions in the warm waters of the Indian Ocean. It remained on her to-do list, along with some similar ambitions that she had thought would never be achieved after splitting up with David.

Now why did he have to come along and ruin everything? Rani stood up and ran the shower, letting the powerful jet pummel her shoulders and loosen the instant tension that those two vowels and three consonants had created in her. She stepped out from the water and wrapped a towel around her head and tied the fluffy guest dressing gown tight in the middle.

From somewhere close inside the house there was a terrific crash. Startled, Rani ran to the bedroom door and straight into the back of Omar, who was looking down the staircase at shards of broken glass. He instinctively put an arm out to stop Rani treading on the pieces.

'Careful, there are bits everywhere.'

She looked at him as he gazed down on all the little shards that covered the steps.

'That'll teach me to carry too much at once, won't it?' he scolded himself and turned to address Rani, but before he spoke again he put a hand up to wipe a drop of water away from her left eye. 'It looks like tears,' he said gently.

Rani dropped her head but didn't shy away from his touch.

'I've just had a bath,' she explained, thinking Omar hadn't noticed.

'The towel on your head, it's a giveaway,' he responded dryly.

'Yes, I suppose so.' Rani struggled to think of anything else to add. His finger was still slowly working its way across her cheek and she felt dizzy and vulnerable. She could feel herself warming to his touch and his presence. Her nakedness was making her feel excited and her chest was starting to blush beneath the bathrobe.

'It's hot in here,' she said pathetically, looking for some way of easing the tension she felt deep inside herself.

'It always feels that way when you've had a hot shower. Anyway, I'm glad to see you're making yourself at home. But don't be too long. I'm cooking tonight.'

Rani was nonplussed by the casualness in Omar's conversation. It seemed so matter-of-fact, so easy-going, so welcoming.

'Great,' she exclaimed. 'And how was your day?' she asked, realising that no sooner had the words left her mouth than she was regretting them.

You daft cow! she said inside her head. *Makes you sound like a married couple!*

Whatever Omar's thoughts on the matter, he kept them to himself and steered the conversation back to his cooking.

'It went well, thank you. I'm doing a chicken recipe I picked up in Lahore. Do you eat chicken?'

'Oh, yes, definitely,' Rani replied, trying to curb her enthusiastic inner-self. 'That would be great. I'll go and get dressed, then. Can't eat in this, can I?'

Omar smiled. But his face didn't give away his thoughts. George arrived at the staircase with a broom and dustpan and began cleaning up the broken fragments of glass.

'Well, then, come to the kitchen when you're ready.'

Rani retreated into the bedroom and quickly shut the door. She really was hot but it had nothing to do with the shower.

You may as well have put a sign up saying come and get it! she admonished herself as she began to dry her hair. Her thoughts began skipping from one thing to another, like a butterfly darting between different flowers, without really settling on anything in particular. After a few minutes she realised she was thinking about the sort of underwear she should put on.

The smell of gently frying onions, garlic and ginger was permeating the house as Rani made her way down the grand staircase towards the kitchen. There, with the sleeves of an obviously very expensive Savile Row shirt rolled up, his hair swept back over his head, his face a study in concentration, was her host and employer. George was sitting at the large kitchen table reading a paper; the sight of Omar Khan chopping and dicing, cutting and slicing food obviously held no fascination for him.

'Can I help?'

Omar looked up and smiled. He was transfixed. Rani looked stunning. She was wearing a tight, figure-hugging dress, and high heels. Her hair was down and flowed around her face, shaping it and defining her. He liked women to look like women with long hair. He had no time for short hair; it didn't matter how good-looking the woman was, it didn't do anything for him. A woman's hair had to touch her shoulders at least. Rani's ticked that box.

'Sure, can you make chapatti?'

'I'm not just a pair of Jimmy Choos, you know. Where's your tava?'

Rani began to knead the flour. Omar looked on without saying anything but taking in every movement of Rani's hands as she expertly made the small pereh ready to cook up for chapatti. When the tava was hot Rani began cooking. Her hands were elegant, with expertly painted nails, but they were also used to the heat of the kitchen. She'd made chapatti and brata a thousand times with her mother. Omar smiled. He could see she was used to the task and that drew him to her. She had an ordinariness that he hadn't really expected from her perfectly pronounced vowels. Rani looked around for a daster khan to put the cooked chapattis in. Omar knew what she was after.

'Bottom right cupboard, just over there.' He pointed towards one of the many cabinets.

If you can judge a man by his bed linen you can certainly judge him on the state of his kitchen ware, Rani thought to herself as she took the well-worn daster khan from the cupboard and began to wrap her chapattis up.

He really did know how to cook and it was more than an example of showing off just for her benefit.

All three tucked into the meal at the kitchen table. There was no pretension, no Egyptian cotton napkins and silver napkin holders, no cut glass or gold cutlery. They ate off domestic, solid Staffordshire plates with their hands. Rani smiled as George kept wiping his between bites and she looked at Omar as he tucked into the food. He had a hunger in him that seemed to rise to the surface in such a sensual act as eating. She stared at him for quite a while, watching how his lips moved and his powerful jaws opened and closed. She found herself drifting off again, being carried away by the moment. Bollywood's number-one hunk was eating the chapattis she had made! How good was that? And he was devouring them, mopping up the curry sauce with them, and it made her feel close to him, worryingly close, stupidly close.

George pushed his plate towards the centre of the table to show he'd had enough. As he licked his lips he spoke.

'Lovely grub. Will there be anything else, Mr Khan?'

Omar was busy cleaning the last of his meal from his plate with the last of the chapatti and just shook his head without looking up.

'No, thanks, George. See you in the morning.'

Rani waited for George to leave the kitchen before speaking.

'That was good.'

Omar looked up; his frowning face showed just how affronted he was.

'Good!'

'OK, it was pretty good,' Rani offered. 'Pretty good, really nice?' She re-inforced her description.

Omar kept looking at Rani, hopeful of getting a better reaction to his cooking.

'OK, it was really nice, very tasty and really good…' she paused before adding '…but not like my mother makes!'

Omar's face went blank. Rani immediately realised what she had said. She'd not meant to say it; it was a natural bragging right to say that your mum's cooking was the best in the world. But not the thing to say to Omar.

'I didn't mean it like that. I'm sorry, I really didn't mean to upset you.'

'You haven't. I just wish I could say the same.'

Rani looked quizzically at him.

'I wish I knew how good my mum's cooking was,' Omar continued. 'I don't even know that about her. She left us when I was really young, my father told me.'

Rani was a little unsure of what to say. If he had been her husband she would have put an arm around him and held him gently, placed a kiss on his neck and waited for his countenance to change. But he certainly wasn't her husband! She hardly knew him, although of course she felt she knew him so well, his public face with the films and newspaper coverage, the gossip and the women with whom he'd been linked. She knew all of that. And in the few days she had spent in close proximity to him she had got to know a little more about his private self, the face the public never saw. He was a fascinating contradiction. Front-page pin-up and multimillionaire playboy, the most powerful man in Indian movies who slept on a mattress on his bedroom floor and who used a battered dasher khan. Rani really wanted to ask him about that, but of course she knew if she did that he would know she had been snooping around. She settled for a compromise.

'You know, you don't have to write this book. I mean, it's not important…' and she paused '…but perhaps, perhaps we can find something out about your mother. Maybe it's a chance, an opportunity for you to discover a little bit more about yourself and where you are from. And you never know, maybe we'll find some people who knew your mother and how well she cooked!'

Rani tried to be as upbeat as possible, unsure how Omar would react. But she needn't have worried.

'Perhaps you're right,' Omar conjectured. 'We should make a proper start tomorrow, if that suits you. I'm off to the set again, not much more to film, but I can point you in the right direction to get you started before I go. Is that OK?'

'Excellent!' Rani uttered, knowing full well it was over-enthusiastic but too late to retract.

'Then let's go to bed,' Omar said.

Rani almost choked on the glass of water she was drinking, spraying it across the table.

Omar realised what he'd said and quickly corrected himself.

'I mean, we've got an early start and perhaps it would be best to get some rest and therefore go to bed—that's what I thought.' He was as embarrassed as Rani and, for a trained actor, stumbled over getting his words out.

'Good idea,' Rani garbled and got up from her chair and fled the room.

'So here I am again!' Rani said, with her lips tight against the duvet. 'Lost in a king-size bed with no king, talking to myself, afraid of myself, afraid of a man. He's just a man!' she told herself.

Oh, but what a man! she thought longingly.

David had been just a man and what a man he had

been too. He had been everything she'd thought she had wanted. She had been taken in by his wonderful good looks, the square jaw and large shoulders, his penetrating eyes and the gentleness of his speech. On the surface he looked the complete package, and training to be a doctor too! Too good to be true. And it was. Far too good to be true. He had proved to be cruel and had treated her emotions with no more consideration than a bowling ball treated a set of skittles. He had knocked her off her feet but heartlessly left her lying there.

At least Omar has helped me to my feet, Rani conjectured.

But despite looking for the silver lining she was afraid. Afraid that history was repeating itself, that her heart was leading her along a path that she had hoped was bathed in the sunshine of the romantic novels she'd read without her parents' knowledge as a teenager, but in fact ended up being drenched in tears. It seemed to be too much. The pain and trauma of investing her emotions and self in another man, and this time a man so beyond all she could ever have expected, was too much. Rejection was for faulty goods, or unsuccessful organ transplants. It wasn't something she ever wanted to experience again. With Omar Khan the fall to earth would be from such a height, if things went wrong, and she expected that they would, that it couldn't possibly be worth the risk. It was utter, sheer, total madness and therefore Rani told herself that she should quit now before things really got out of hand. As she slipped into sleep she had made her mind up that the following morning she was going to come clean to Omar and admit she couldn't stay with him to write his autobiography.

* * *

Rani didn't sleep well. She woke with thoughts completely contrary to those she'd had eight hours earlier. During the night her subconscious had obviously convinced her that it wasn't all bad being so close to such a man, and that she was much older than she'd been when she'd been left so devastated by David that now she could handle any situation. She was older, wiser, tougher, and anyway she'd always wanted to write a book and she wasn't going to give up just because she might have the hots for the leading man!

With that resolution set firmly in her mind she showered, dressed and made her way to face the cause of her current predicament. She needn't have worried. He wasn't there. Her heart sank and rose at the same time. She didn't have to meet him but she wanted to. There was no sign of George either. She was alone in the house. As she made herself a cup of tea Rani realised the time—it was past nine and they had obviously left for the film set. As she opened the fridge to get some milk she instantly saw the note stuck to the carton.

'We left early. Didn't want to wake you. Make yourself at home—the office is all yours. Omar.'

And there was a PS.

'You looked so peaceful. One all.'

It took a moment for the words to sink in.

How did he know I looked so peaceful? Rani mused. *He must have peeked at me while I was asleep!*

'Pervert!' she said out loud, laughing as she poured the hot water into her mug. He had obviously realised, or more likely been told by George, that she had poked her nose into his bedroom so he had returned the favour.

One all—a draw; I could settle for that, Rani thought. She made herself some toast and wandered around the house, safe in the knowledge that she really was alone and it was unlikely she'd be disturbed. It was a liberating feeling, trusted to be alone with all the priceless artefacts, and more important left alone to rummage if she dared to. Ordinarily perhaps she might have done if she didn't have the feelings for her host that she did, but, having been caught once, and knowing she was finding it hard to control herself, she thought better of it. Proud of herself, Rani headed to the office where she found stacks of paper, boxes of pens and notebooks and anything else that Omar had obviously thought she might need. The room looked like a stationer's. That made her smile. It also made her happy that she'd made the right decision and not taken advantage of being left alone in an Aladdin's cave of what could easily be turned into fan memorabilia on the Internet or a thieves' open house.

Returning from her bedroom with her laptop, Rani began to arrange the office in a way that suited her. It was orderly and workmanlike. She was pleased with herself and rewarded her efforts with a pot of tea. She spent the day making a start on the piles of cuttings and documents inside the filing cabinets. Much of it she had already seen. Omar had obviously had a cuttings agency monitor what was said about him and kept a record of it. There were reviews of his films, which Rani read with an objective mind, and there were various snippets of tittle-tattle gossip about him and many different women that she found herself rereading and couldn't be as detached from. She was partway though one of those stories when she felt the presence of someone else in the room. She turned with a start and a racing heart to find Omar standing behind her. She gasped with shock and relief.

'How long have you been there?'

'Oh, not too long. Just long enough to see you trace your fingers under that woman's name a couple of times.'

'That's unfair; you've been spying on me!'

'Not spying, just checking up.'

'I call it spying, and anyway you almost scared me to death, creeping up behind me like that.'

'You look very much alive to me,' Omar replied.

'That's not the point! What if I'd been doing something else?'

'Like what?'

'Oh, I don't know—something more personal.'

'What could be more personal? You're in my office, reading my things!'

Rani wouldn't be beaten.

'Personal things. You seemed happy enough to sneak into my bedroom and watch me sleep, didn't you?'

That caught Omar off guard. He'd been having the better of their jousting but Rani's allusion to his note was unexpected.

Rani was enjoying the verbal sparring. It was risqué. There was an element of danger in it, the chance it might go too far, and she liked that. It seemed the more she put up resistance to the way she felt, the more the naughty devil on her shoulder liked it. It was turning her on.

'I was just seeing if you were going to be available for a breakfast meeting,' Omar said in his defence, 'but it was pretty clear by how much you were snoring that you were fast asleep.'

'I don't snore,' Rani protested. 'I don't snore, do I?' she asked, a little unsure now of just exactly what it was she was talking about.

Omar thought about taking the joke further, but, remembering how he had joked at her expense when they had first met, he thought better of it.

'Well, OK, I made that bit up, about the snoring. I don't really know—after all, I only put my head round the door. It's not like I spent the night with you.'

It was all getting a little too close to the bone for both of them but it was as if they were locked in a spiral of innuendo, each unable to extract themselves from the situation. Fortunately the phone in the office rang. Making them both jump a little, and cutting off their verbal tennis mid-game. Rani instinctively reached out to pick up the receiver as Omar bent over her to do the same. Their hands touched and the initial spark Rani had felt when Omar had helped her up from the pavement crackled like electricity around her body. She momentarily felt so faint it was fortunate she was already sitting down.

'Sorry,' Rani whispered as she handed the phone to Omar.

He began talking to the caller while at the same time writing a note on a pad in front of him.

Ten minutes in my house and you think it's yours!

Rani read it and snorted to herself. The tennis match was back on. She wrote a quick reply.

Well, you did say treat it as my own! And she drew a little smiling face to emphasise the point. Omar was definitely paying more attention to what Rani was doing than he was on his call.

'Sorry, can you repeat that, please?' he asked the anonymous voice on the other end of the conversation.

Rani was wondering just what would happen next—what did she dare do? Omar was standing so close to her, his award-winning bottom just an inch away from her. She was overcome with a desire to grab it in both hands. It seemed like an eternity as her mind played out the consequences of such a brazen assault; so overwhelmed was she by the image that she was unsure if she'd actually made a move or not. She snapped back from her daydream as Omar replaced the phone. His hand brushed against hers. It was too deliberate to have been an accident. With the anticipation of his presence but unsure of what was happening, Rani continued to look straight out in front, not daring to even sneak a peek out of the corner of her eye.

'Stand up,' he asked her gently.

It was a polite request and Rani obliged. All her senses were on a hair trigger waiting for his touch. She knew she had been waiting for him to hold her properly since he had first offered his hand to her, and now she was eager for the moment to come and at the same time so fearful and nervous. Rani felt the warmth of his skin on her hands and looked down to see his large hands covering hers. He gently ran his hands up her forearms and her upper arms to her shoulders. Her back winced at his touch and she felt a surge in her body, which couldn't be turned off. As Omar massaged her shoulders and arms she felt his lips kiss the back of her head. Repeatedly his lips kissed her, each time they got nearer to her neck. It was like torture waiting for his next move, urging it along, and finally he kissed the bare skin and sent a shiver out from that one delicately placed kiss to her whole body. His hands left her shoulders and cupped her breasts as he expertly placed more kisses across her neck. Rani relaxed into his arms enjoying the moment as his hands found a way into her blouse and touched her breasts. She let out a small gasp as first the left and then the right hand began to stroke and tease her nipples. His touch was gentle and expert. Rani turned her head and found his mouth. She took charge, kissing him firmly on the lips. His mouth yielded to hers as she kissed him again and again. Omar lowered his head onto her exposed breasts and began to kiss and bite her nipples, switching his attention from one to the other. Rani closed her eyes, her head swaying with the feelings of ecstasy that flowed around every inch of her body. She was waiting for him to move his hands lower; she wanted him to inch his fingers down her body, which was aching to be touched. He got the message and his hands worked back down her waist and round her bottom. Rani felt wanton, spreading her legs as far as the skirt she was wearing would allow. Omar took the hint and ran his hands all over her rear until he found the zip. He hesitated for a moment.

'Yes,' Rani said, giving him free rein to take advantage as her skirt fell to the floor of the office. She breathed deeper and faster as she felt Omar's hands glide across her skin. She had never experienced such uncontrollable feelings. Her head spun in a dizzy confusion of delight, danger and desire. She couldn't control her own body as it responded with a shuddering, irrepressible wave of ecstasy to Omar's touch.

CHAPTER EIGHT

'THAT WAS NICE,' Rani said in a low soft voice.

'What was?'

'That thing you did!' She giggled.

'What thing?' Omar was pulling her leg.

'You know! That thing! The thing you just did! Do I have to spell it out for you?' Rani rolled over in the bed to face the living reality of the poster that had once looked down upon her from her own bedroom wall. She smiled and touched the rough stubble on his face. It hadn't been a dream. Of course it hadn't. This was the real deal, the main event and she had to adjust to it. She had finally given in to the feelings she'd known were growing inside her heart from the first moment he'd helped her up from the pavement. She'd promised herself never to head along this road again and here she was, only this time it wasn't a good-looking, rugby-playing doctor she'd let into her heart, it was Omar Khan, *the* Omar Khan. The man a million women would promise never to buy another pair of shoes again if only they could trade places with her.

Just how many women have been in this place? The thought darted through Rani's head. She forced it out. It wasn't something she wanted to think about. She was with him now and in her mind she was the only woman to be there, now and for ever. She edged closer to him and put her arms out to cuddle his smooth body. She knew now she wanted to give herself completely to him. But surprisingly he recoiled.

'Later,' he said rather abruptly, as if something was agitating him. 'I've some business to get on with.' And he rolled out of the bed leaving Rani suddenly alone. She watched as he dressed quickly.

'Don't be long,' she called out after him.

Omar turned and gave her half a smile and was gone. Disappointed at being abandoned so soon after deciding that this was *the* man, Rani got up and quickly gathered her clothes before sneaking out of Omar's room and back to her own far more luxurious suite.

He really is a complicated set of contradictions, she thought to herself as she enjoyed the hospitality of the enormous shower. As ever the warmth of a shower and comfort of a piping hot cup of tea banished the doubts Rani had. She had given herself to him willingly. She'd resisted the temptation for as long as she could, until she knew it was right, and she had known. She was convinced of that. All the emotions that had twisted and tumbled inside her, the feelings of doubt, the fears and recollections of her vulnerability and the possibility of repeating a mistake like David, had played their part. Each had been judged and weighed by her rationalism and in the end she dismissed it all, going instead with the feeling in her heart. The ache that told her she was truly in love with Omar Khan. At that moment she gave in to herself.

There was no sign of Omar in the kitchen, nor any note or message left for her. Neither was there any trace of the perpetually loyal George. It looked very much as if Rani had been left home alone again.

'Ah, well,' she told the kettle. 'It looks like it's just you and me again. Would I like a cup? What a great idea, thank you!'

Armed with a pot of tea on a tray, she made her way to the office. After all, she thought, she was there to do a job, and distractions like making love to her employer were taking her mind off the task! The morning seemed to go quickly as Rani rooted around the large bundles of papers. It was becoming clear to her that she'd have to impose more order on all the different things she was finding and so a dozen different piles of paper soon began to grow. A sticky label identified what they related to.

'Not bad!' she said, admiring the system she'd established. 'I'll just do these and then get some lunch.' She had a small bundle of brown envelopes in her hand. They looked unimportant, abandoned almost, but were all tied together with a thin pink ribbon. Rani casually undid the knot holding them in place and, without taking much notice, scanned the front for any signs of what they might contain. There was nothing written on any of them. No indication of what they might contain. Rani began paying more attention and shook the contents of each one out. They looked like documents. She couldn't tell; the writing wasn't English.

'Urdu?' she questioned, and she turned the thin pages over and saw the official-looking seals and stamps. Her eyes scanned along the lines, adjusting to the script. It had been a very long time since she had read anything in Urdu and she struggled to make much sense of it. She darted across the page looking for familiar words. She pulled more papers from the other envelopes, looking for further clues to what she'd found. And then it struck her just what she'd discovered. Down on her hands and knees, frantically she twisted and turned every scrap of paper she could find. Her heart was racing and her mouth had gone instantly dry as a sense of panic spread through her entire body.

'Hi, Rani, I'm back. How are you doing?' It was Omar.

Rani was in a daze.

'I said hi.' Omar put his head into the office, and when he saw Rani on the carpet his voice became more concerned. 'What is it? Are you all right?'

'Well, for one thing, you left me this morning, alone, in your bed, if you hadn't noticed! What is it? Was I not good enough?'

'Hey,' Omar cried out quickly. 'It was nothing like that, really it wasn't. I just—'

'Just what? Had a better offer?' she interrupted him.

Omar was shocked by the frosty welcome, but perhaps he deserved it. After all, he had gone off rather quickly that morning; he hadn't actually explained properly to Rani, but how could he? Would she understand how he was starting to feel about her? For once, for perhaps the first time in his life, he had stopped himself—stopped himself taking advantage of the situation, of having what he wanted because of who and what he was. He had had to leave her, to get away from his own desire for her. He knew that if he had remained just one minute longer next to her beautiful and naked body he would have regretted it, because he wanted it to be different this time. It had to be different this time because she was so very special. How was he going to be able to explain that to Rani? That he was rejecting her to save himself for the right moment!

Rani didn't say anything as she twisted towards him, clutching the papers in her hands, waving them towards him. Omar's face instantly changed from smiles to stone as he realised what she held. Still Rani remained quiet.

'Oh, is that all?' Omar tried to joke the matter off but his voice betrayed his concern. 'That's nothing,' he continued, but he was in a dead end.

Rani pushed herself to her feet and waved the papers again.

'I would hardly call it nothing. When were you going to tell me, eh?'

'Tell you what? It's not important, really.' Omar was struggling.

'Not important!' Rani's voice began to crack. 'What would you call important, then? Tell me that!' She pushed the papers ahead of herself as she walked towards him.

'Really, Rani, it was so long ago. I was seventeen. I'd forgotten all about it.'

'Forgotten! How could you forget something like that?' she protested. 'Why did you keep the papers if you'd "forgotten". Let me remind you, then, shall I?'

'There's no need.'

'No need! Just when were you going to tell me that you were married?'

Omar gave a nervous, edgy laugh.

'It's no joking matter. I'm surprised you find it so funny.' Her tone changed. He wasn't taking her concerns seriously and that was not the way she was used to being treated.

'What do you think's going on here, Rani?' He was half smiling at her. He could see it was getting her more wound up and he continued with it. 'It's not important—it's nothing. Things aren't always as they seem,' he said.

'Really, you're taking it all too seriously. I mean, you're not my wife.'

'No, no, I'm not. But this woman is! Whoever she is or wherever she is! Isn't she? If I was your wife I wouldn't let you treat me this way.'

'What's that supposed to mean?'

'Work it out. After all, you're the one who knows just how to make any woman tick—isn't that what it said in the article I wrote? God, how wrong was I? You had me for a fool. Go on, then, tell me—what makes me tick, Mr Omar Khan?'

'You're just like all the others,' he began. His face was growing angrier with every word that left his mouth. 'Not really seeing me for who I am and only after one thing!'

'Others!' Rani retorted angrily. She could give as good as she got and to be lumped together with every gold-digging tart that had ever kept his bed warm was not something she was prepared to stand for.

'Yes, others,' Omar barked back. 'Every one of them, all of you, all of you want a slice of me, a piece of the "great Omar Khan, Bollywood legend", to stick in the scrapbook or boast about to your friends. Well, I'm not putting up with it from you! Do you hear me?'

'Oh, I hear very well.' Rani took another step towards him. The blood was boiling in her veins. The cheek of this man, to think she needed his money or his fame. 'You arrogant pig. How dare you even talk about me and all of your other tarts in the same breath? As if I would need your money! It was you that asked me to work for you, remember. You wanted a favour from me, and you only bought my writing skills, nothing else. Do *you* hear *me*? Nothing else was, or is, or ever would be for sale to you or any man. You can go to hell.'

She was filled with an anger so passionate that she would not let go of it. She had decided to invest all of herself into their relationship and this was how that valuable treasure was rewarded. If that was the case then he would hear every word she wanted to speak.

'You think I need you! You think I need your fame to make a name for myself! Ha, that's a joke! I was doing very well, thank you, before you came along. I was happy.' She knew it was a half-truth as she said it but she wasn't going to give Omar any satisfaction in knowing just how much he had got under her skin, just how much she wanted him. She always had been prepared to cut her nose off to spite her face and this moment was no exception. Rani was on the offensive and with each verbal jab she made at Omar she jabbed her finger, taking a step closer each time until he was on the retreat. Eventually she paused for breath.

'So you can order me a taxi right this minute!'

Stunned for a moment, Omar took a minute to respond.

'Fine, I will.'

'Fine,' replied Rani.

'Good!'

'I'll do it right now!'

'Good! Go on, then!'

'Good!' Omar stormed off and left Rani to go to her room and start collecting her things into one of her cases. She ran her arm along the dressing table, sweeping up the various make-up, face creams and brushes she'd so carefully laid out and thrust all her clothes into another case haphazardly.

Ten minutes later she was sitting in the back of the taxi heading away from Omar's country mansion, her head a complete tangled mess of thoughts.

'Ah!' she screamed suddenly.

The taxi driver slammed on the brake in an emergency stop.

'What is it, love?'

Rani had remembered her favourite lipstick. She'd left it behind.

'Oh, nothing. I'm sorry—please keep going.'

She rested her head in her hands and leant against the cold window of the taxi. Rani closed her eyes hoping it would all go away. How stupid she had been. How naive to think that there were no skeletons in Omar's cupboards. How hurt she felt. After she'd broken up with David she had promised herself never to set herself up to fall so far ever again. That was why she had always kept her distance from men, always kept her heart safe and out of harm's way. Now here she was reliving an almost perfect rerun of that awful time. Tears gently seeped from her eyes and began to run down her cheeks. She was broken-hearted.

Omar wasn't sure where he was going to drive to or why. It was just a need within him. A need to do something, to be heading somewhere. A need not to be still and contemplating the things that he knew would jump into his head if he let them. In cases like these it was always better to be on the move. He watched the road as the headlights picked out the curve ahead of him. He drove without thinking, looking into the hedgerows and occasionally spotting a rabbit beside the verge. He had no desire to run them down so he slowed as he passed, hoping he wouldn't startle them. He crossed the junction that led towards the motorway and automatically joined the carriageway north. He went with the flow, turned on the CD player and hit the random play function. He didn't want to control what he was going to listen to.

As he approached the ring road around Manchester he finally knew where he was going even if he didn't want to admit it to himself. He preferred to think of it as an accidental choice but really he knew it wasn't. The traffic was light, most people were heading out of the city as he drove in and through it, towards Longsight. He slowed down to look up at the skyline, which he noted had changed so much since he had roamed the streets as a young lad. Omar began to contemplate change and age and the things that went with it, like responsibility and settling down. What right did she have to question what he'd done all those years ago? *Typical woman, no sooner in your bed than running your life!* For more than an hour and a half he had successfully blocked her from his mind, but then without warning and quite uninvited she popped back into it. The calm he had felt driving vaporised in that instant. He pulled over towards the kerb and turned the engine off. He grabbed his jacket and got out.

The streets were almost deserted. They were a series of narrow roads that combined to make up his old stomping ground. As a boy he'd run and played and thought nothing of the place. It had been home, the rows of tightly built houses, the low-rise blocks of flats with their fenced-in play areas. The pubs were still there and the dozens of Pakistani and Bangladeshi restaurants, the clothes factories and the funny little shops that seemed to appear wherever there was a large immigrant community, selling flights and mobile phone cards so people could stay in contact with the country they'd left behind. He wasn't sure why he'd returned, or where he was heading; it just seemed like a necessary thing to do.

'Stuck up busybody,' he said to himself as he thought of Rani's initial reaction to the place. She frustrated him so much it made his blood boil. With her perfect manners and perfectly pronounced vowels. *And the perfect body, don't forget the perfect body, and the smile, oh, her wonderful smile.* As much as he tried to be angry with Rani he kept thinking about her smile and her nakedness; she was the most perfect woman he had ever seen on every level and that made it so much worse. Without realising it Omar found himself standing in front of the Gardener's Arms pub, which sat on an apex of two narrow streets running from the high street. He'd not been into a pub for years—culturally it wasn't his sort of place, and now he looked down his nose on them as grimy and dirty venues full of life's riff-raff.

He pushed the door open and stepped inside. His club in London was the complete antithesis to the Gardener's Arms. Where his club had marble floors, the pub had old stained carpets, soggy with beer and burnt through with years of stubbed-out cigarettes. Where his club had luxurious, deep leather seating, the pub had wooden benches and stiff, hard chairs on heavy cast-iron legs. It was after midnight but a hard core of regulars were still drinking; their voices were loud and slurred. Their heads turned slowly and collectively towards the door and the stranger who had dared enter. The air was short of oxygen but heavy with stale smoke and flat beer. Omar didn't feel apprehensive or overpowered by the cautious and wary welcome. He came from the streets surrounding the pub and knew how to behave and how to respond. It was like falling off a log and he blended in within moments. By the time he'd reached the bar his body movement and facial expression showed he was a local.

'Spud!' a familiar voice called out from the back of the pub.

'Digger?'

'Yeah, of course it's me.'

'What are you doing here?'

'Shouldn't I be asking you that?' Digger said in his usual exuberant style. 'After all, it's my local. I don't know, haven't seen you since we were lads, you've not stepped inside this postcode for twenty years, I reckon, and here you are twice in almost as many days. What's going on?'

It was a very good question and one Omar had been asking himself many times. What was he doing back here among the streets, the buildings, the people he'd tried so hard to forget?

'What's the matter—you got homesick or something?' Digger enjoyed making jokes, especially at Omar's expense. The two young women he was with were obviously drunk and giggling along with him. 'Come on, sit yourself down. What'll you have?'

Omar walked towards the table. He could feel the stickiness of the carpet beneath his feet. *Is this home?* he thought to himself. *Have I been round in a circle and ended up back where I started from?*

'Ladies, let me introduce Mr Omar Khan, but you can call him Spud.'

Omar nodded to the women.

'Once an upstanding member of the local community, now for his sins no longer of this parish. Let me hear the congregation say Amen!'

Digger continued as he was enjoying pulling the leg

of his old friend. The women joined in on the Amen and Digger kept talking.

'Yes, brothers and sisters, Spud 'ere was taken from us from at an early age and transformed from boyhood lout and tearaway into the multimillionaire film star you see before you! Spud, may I introduce Chloe and Chelsea?'

Everyone in the pub was listening by now and they all burst into laughter. None of them believed a word that came from Digger's mouth. Normally with good reason—he had a reputation for dodgy stories and dodgy deals.

'You're kiddin', ain't yer?' Chelsea asked Digger.

'Cross my heart and hope to wake up next to you! No, I ain't! He's a bonifi…a bonifid…a kosher megastar.'

'Is 'e tellin' the truth?' Chloe asked, looking up into Omar's eyes.

'I act a bit, that's true,' he said coolly.

'Hasn't he got the most wonderful coloured eyes?' she stated. 'Are they contact lenses?'

'All God's gift,' Omar said. He could charm the birds from the trees, so a couple of tipsy women were no problem.

'If you're so famous, 'own come I don't know yer?' asked Chelsea, her head now resting in her hand, itself supported by a rather wobbly elbow on the table.

'I act in Indian films. You know—Bollywood,' Omar said, rather bored with the conversation. He looked at Digger, at what he had become in all the years they had wandered their separate ways, and he saw nothing but the past. Digger was still the same person he'd left behind all those years ago. His face was more lined, the youthfulness sucked from it by time; his hair was still a mess but now graying and he had put on weight. But beneath the external changes, he was still the same, chatting to the girls, ducking and diving, sometimes straying a little too close to the boundaries of what was legal. He'd been born a stone's throw from the pub and it was pretty clear he was going to die close to it without ever experiencing the outside world.

'You'd have seen him in that latest one with, what's-his-name—you know, *On Target*,' Digger suggested. It was true Omar had had a supporting role in a blockbuster; crossing over from Bollywood to Hollywood wasn't easy but he was trying to. His face was better known to tens of millions more people than his tinsel town co-stars, but, in Hollywood, Indian films counted for nothing.

'Oh, yes, 'e does look familiar now you mention it. You played the evil bloke, didn't you?'

Omar nodded and then spoke.

'And before you ask, yes, he's much shorter in real life.'

'He's a flipping' mind-reader an' all!' exclaimed Chelsea.

'Digger, can I have a word?' Omar asked.

'Excuse me, ladies,' Digger said as he slid along the bench and stood up next to Omar. 'Walk into my office,' he said, pointing to the end of the bar beside a fruit machine. 'What can I get you?'

'No, it's my shout, let me, and what are they on?' Omar said, indicating towards Chloe and Chelsea.

'Anything that looks and tastes remotely like white wine will go down a treat. I'll just have a top up in that.' He handed Omar a glass that had obviously contained whiskey. 'So why are you here? Come to see how the other half live?'

'Something like that,' Omar began, and then ordered

the drinks. 'A bottle of the best white you've got, fill this up, please,' he said, handing Digger's glass over, 'and I'll have a tomato juice, with Worcestershire Sauce and ice, thanks.'

Omar turned from the bar and looked out across the pub. He wasn't really sure why he was there. He'd felt defensive of the place, of the people and the buildings, when he'd walked around with Rani. Maybe that was just because he thought she was looking down her nose or maybe it was his own guilt at having got away and not really wanting to come back. He'd hidden it away. Just like the marriage documents that Rani had found. Was it the same as he'd left it, when he'd been taken to Pakistan by his father? At first sight it had seemed it. On this second visit that suspicion was confirmed. Nothing had really changed, despite the millions of pounds spent on redevelopment—none of the money had made its way this far from the city centre.

'I'm not sure why I'm here, Digger,' Omar said, resuming the conversation when the drinks arrived. 'Perhaps I wanted it to be the same, to feel I could connect with it, and it's true—it looks pretty much the same as it was. You certainly do!' he said, patting Digger on the shoulder. 'Still the same old Digger trying it on with the ladies. Isn't it time you got married and had a family?'

Digger looked momentarily offended.

'Been there, tried it and got the T-shirt and the kids and the ex to prove it! It wasn't for me. I'm obviously not the marrying kind.' He joked at his own misfortune. 'But it's not too bad—the kids are great.'

'How many?'

'Three, one of each!' Digger joked. 'Nah, two boys and a girl, all going their own way now. The eldest has just started university; she's a great kid. As for the boys, who knows? You know what it's like around here. You need a break to get ahead, don't you?'

He was philosophical and realistic. It was hard making something of yourself when the opportunities weren't given to you on a plate. That was what Rani didn't or wouldn't understand, Omar thought to himself. The harsh reality of having to go without food because there was a bill to pay or of having the electricity cut off because you had to buy food. The people round here were trapped by their situation and only those that learnt to swim would rise to the top while the others would sink back to the bottom of the pond. Being forced to marry because you really had no other option, just so your greedy father could get his hands on a dowry.

Omar finished his drink and reached into his pocket for the money clip he had been nursing there. He palmed it without Digger seeing.

'OK, Digger, that's me finished. It was good to see you again.' And he went to shake his hand, leaving the thick wedge of money in his friend's hand. 'Take care of yourself. Take care of your children.' Before Digger could say anything Omar headed for the door and back out into the quiet of the early morning. Digger looked at the present left in his upturned hand: a large silver and diamond clip stretched wide open by the number of notes it held. He looked shocked by the amount it must have held, and then went back towards the bar and ordered another drink.

Omar strolled back to his BMW. His mind was fitting the jigsaw pieces together even though he was tired. He had been drawn back to where he had been born out of necessity, out of a desire to experience it just once more. The longer he thought about it, the more he realised that it hadn't altered at all. It was he who had changed. From the moment he'd flown out of Heathrow, sitting next to his father, to a land he'd known nothing about, he was changed for ever. He'd experienced an entirely different culture and way of being and it had opened his eyes to the world without him realising it. The struggle he'd had to endure to make it, the effort he'd put into creating a career for himself, had been in order to escape his past, and if there had been any romantic notion that it was worth revisiting that had now been laid to rest. He might still be able to fit in among the inhabitants but he was no longer truly one of them. He couldn't be, not again, and there was no point in looking back. He had to carve out a future as he'd carved out a career. And as he thought about the future he thought about Rani.

CHAPTER NINE

CONSIDERING HOW SHE was feeling, Rani was surprised she had fallen asleep on the long journey back to her little flat in London. She only awoke as the driver turned the engine off and gently roused her. She reached for her purse.

'No need, love. All paid for.'

Rani was taken aback by that. *At least he got something right,* she thought as she blinked and shook her head in an effort to come to.

'You take it easy, love.' The driver spoke as she headed towards the entrance, dragging her bag behind her. 'Take my advice—you make yourself a nice warm cupper!'

Rani thanked him and smiled. *Do I look that bad?* she thought as she rode in the lift to her front door. The flat seemed cold and a little strange after the vastness of Omar's mansion but it felt good to be surrounded by her own things. A familiar surrounding was always important if you wanted to feel safe. But for once she didn't flick the kettle on; she was too tired, and wearily Rani headed to bed. It was a little after midnight. At first she felt cold and alone beneath the duvet but her mind didn't trouble her for long. She was physically and emotionally exhausted and drifted off to sleep. With no alarm to wake her in the morning she slept until it was past eleven o'clock.

'Today is a new day!' she said to herself as she lay in bed looking at the ceiling. She felt like being positive, like taking charge and making her own destiny and not being pushed and battered along like a piece of flotsam in the surf. Rani began mentally counting her blessings, family and friends, the break from work, the opportunity to write a book and the lucky escape from a deceitful boyfriend. Whenever one part of her life wasn't going the way she hoped she would throw all her energies into another aspect of it. When she'd struggled to find the job she was after she'd concentrated on making herself a more desirable catch for would-be employers by making sure her CV was beefed up. She'd taken on voluntary work to show she was caring and in touch with society and she'd worked hard on finding exclusive stories she could get published as a freelancer. When she'd broken up with David she'd joined the gym and trained long and hard enough to enter a marathon.

This time it was going to be harder. She didn't have work to console her and she couldn't confide in her parents. The only outlet on which to concentrate was the book and of course that was all about HIM! This time it was going to be tough. But Rani told herself that if she could get through this, then she'd be able to get through anything. *Think of it as just a job.* And she wrote it down on pieces of paper that she stuck up around the house. *It's just a job!* But that was never the whole truth and Rani knew it, no matter how hard she tried to convince herself.

For the first couple of weeks, it was a real struggle. She just couldn't iron out the turmoil she felt, but when an interesting lead about Omar's mother took her out of the flat to do some research at the public records office Rani found she was able to shift her focus, and her journalistic instincts for a story overcame the Omar-shaped hurdles that had been blocking her way.

But it was hard to block him out. Impossible, in fact—after all, the book she was researching was all about him! Here she was, full of anger and hurt from the top of her head to her toes, having to dig around in his past and try to remain detached and unaffected. She was being pulled in all directions by her feelings. She didn't know whether to get in a taxi and head straight to Omar's house so she could give him a slap on the face or a kiss. She wanted to call him, to hear his voice. She wanted to tell him to his face what she thought of him, his arrogant attitude to her and dismissing her concerns about his teenage marriage. She wanted to hurt him as she was hurting. She wanted to be in his arms again, to be held tightly by him, to hear what he had to say and to make love to him again. Each time she rolled over in the bed and began drifting off to sleep another thought would prick her awake until she gave up even attempting to get any rest. Instead she propped herself up in the bed, switched on the television for a bit of company and began making a list. As always she drew up two columns: one she labeled *For* and the other, *Against*.

She chewed the end of the pen as she deliberated what should be placed beneath each heading. Compiling the list this time was easier than the last time she had tried weighing up the pros and cons of allowing Omar Khan into her life. Under *For* she began with *I love him*. There was no denying it; no matter how she felt about him right now, she knew she really did love him. Then added, *great eyes, great lover, wealthy, handsome, funny* and the list continued until the page was almost full.

'This one's for Shilpa,' Rani said out loud as she added, *he hasn't got a saggy bottom* to the list.

'Now for the *Against*,' Rani said. *This should be even easier* she thought to herself, and began with *he's married, he lied to me*. But then she paused and thought. He hadn't ever told her he wasn't married, had he? And she had never asked him if he was married, had she? So he hadn't actually lied about being married. Rani crossed that out. Instead she wrote, *deceitful*. Next she added *my Mum and Dad*, and then, *does he want me?* and she finished with *getting hurt*. It might have been a short list but it gave Rani plenty to think about. Her parents were always going to be an issue; it didn't matter who she wanted to date. Parents, fathers especially, never liked seeing their daughters with men, full stop. At the very least any husband material needed to be a consultant, preferably in brain or heart surgery and certainly with their own private practice. They were the sorts of candidates her father had introduced her to in the past. Even then, with impeccable credentials, the cleanest fingernails and most highly polished shoes, no man would be deserving enough of Rani's hand in marriage for her father! So a man who acted for a living, an entertainer, and one with a reputation, well, he would have no chance!

But did Omar actually want her back and on what terms? That was hard to tell. They'd not spoken for more than two weeks now, and her last words to him were, 'Go to hell.' She cringed now when she thought about them. *Perhaps he's over me, perhaps he was never into me in the first place. What was it that he said? I was just like all the others. Perhaps I gave him just the get-*

out he was after, she thought. *But what about the book? He wanted me to do the book.*

And so she had carried on working on it, despite their estrangement. Doubts and more doubts, possible solutions and answers tumbled in, one on top of another, until Rani felt she'd have to draw up another list of reasons he'd want to be with her. But that just made her feel more unhappy and she decided to accept that fate would decree what the outcome would be. She immediately looked around her bedroom for that day's newspaper and flicked through the pages looking for the horoscopes.

'Err, well, I suppose you can read that a couple of ways,' she said, convincing herself that everything written in papers—horoscopes especially—wasn't always as it seemed.

'That's what he said about the marriage certificate!' Rani gasped. 'Oh, I was so stupid. I should have listened to him. I should have given him time to explain, but, oh, no, I put my big foot in it and told him to go to hell. Well done, Rani!'

She looked at the last entry beneath the *Against* heading: *getting hurt*. Restraining herself from speaking out loud again, Rani began drumming her fingers on the back of the television remote control instead, while her mind tried to order a logical argument against worrying about getting hurt. *Getting hurt is part of being a human being*, she began. *So far so good. We fall over and graze our knees, we fall off swings, we fall off our bikes, our pets die and our relatives die. We get hurt in different ways and to different degrees. Being hurt in love is just one way, it's rarely terminal and can be treated by large doses of soppy movies, girlfriends, pizza and white wine!* Then she thought of the words her riding instructor had used all those years ago when she was just a little girl and was afraid after falling from a horse.

'Get yourself back up in the saddle; you'll never learn how to ride sitting on the ground.'

It was true and the instructor had said nothing more; she hadn't fussed over Rani as she sat in the sawdust of the training arena. She matter-of-factly told her to get on with it and didn't even ask her if she was all right. Her attitude was that falling off horses was bound to happen so you might as well accept it. It was an occupational hazard. Having your heart broken was a part of falling in love. It didn't mean it had to happen every time but it could. It was one of the possible consequences of romance. Not everyone who rode a horse fell off every time; in fact it wasn't that common, but it did happen. The same was true of love. Just because you got hurt once didn't mean it was destined to happen again. It just might. And you would never know unless you tried.

Rani knew perfectly well what she was doing. She was convincing herself that she was going to have to return to Omar. She was going to have to face him, whatever the consequences. After all, she'd signed a contract to ghost-write his autobiography and the first installment of her retainer had arrived from the publishers. She wasn't going to renege on the deal, but nor was she about to make the same mistakes again. First and foremost she and Omar had a business arrangement. The fact that they had made love just complicated things. But Rani wasn't the sort of woman to back away from a challenge or opportunity and writing the book was the biggest opportunity she had been given. She was going to grab it with both hands and hold onto it as if her life depended on it. Her parents were always worried about her; they couldn't help themselves. That was what parents did, especially hers. They didn't know anything about how intimate she and Omar had been and they would never need to. It was a one-off, a mistake that she had made, and not one she was going to repeat. For the first time in ages Rani felt strong, really strong, as if she had looked into the face of a terrifying fate and overcome it. Omar Khan might have taken advantage of her, but she accepted she'd also taken advantage of him and was still going to. She had a book to write and he was her major source of material so she could hardly get the project finished without going back to see him. But this time it would be on her terms and there would be no repeat of their previous encounter, she promised herself as she packed her case.

'Nice to see you again, Miss de Silver,' George said as he met Rani at the railway station.

She had been the only passenger to get off at the quiet rural stop and it had taken Rani quite a bit of organising to ensure she chose the right service and coordinate its arrival with George.

'You know, I would have come and collected you from London if you'd asked.'

'I know, George, but I am an independent woman. I can make my own way in life.'

Rani was determined to show her new self off and she wasn't sure what George knew about her night with Omar, if anything. Whatever he knew she was determined to show her business side and not be reliant on Omar for anything but information and interviews. She was throwing herself into her work, convincing herself there were no issues that needed to be resolved. Even on the train journey out of London Rani had managed to contain the emotions inside her and had done a pretty good job of convincing herself that she didn't need Omar Khan in her life, nor did she have any feelings for him. She'd told herself to behave and to stick firmly to some guiding principles about their relationship. It was to be grown-up, mature and businesslike. She had identified two areas of conversation to stick to and these were the book and the weather. Everything else was strictly out of bounds and she would steer any conversation towards them.

Rani had also decided to keep the amount of time she spent in Omar's company to an absolute minimum. That meant she was no longer going to have meals with him, watch television with him, and she certainly wasn't going to spend any time—except for interviews—alone with him, especially not in the cinema, sauna or any bedroom! She reasoned that if she stuck rigidly to the protocols then there would be no risk of a repeat of their lovemaking.

Omar wasn't at home when Rani arrived. No amount of repeating self-help mantras was going to prepare her for the first encounter so she was relieved to be able to enter the house and reinstall herself in the same guest room undisturbed. Once she'd unpacked Rani headed for the office. It was as she had left it: the piles of papers were still stacked on the floor, the notebook she had been using before her hasty departure lay open on the desk. The only thing missing seemed to be the paperwork she'd thrown at Omar as she'd stormed out.

'Research only, Rani de Silver,' she said in a stern voice to no one but herself. 'You are here to work, take the money, put your name on the cover and get out!'

Omar didn't return to the mansion that evening nor the next day or the next. He was busy on the set and stayed in the trailer. By the time George collected him at the end of the week Rani had settled into a rhythm of work that was suiting her. She sent emails and made calls on her research in the morning and sorted papers, indexed material and wrote in the afternoon. Even if she looked organised from the outside she still felt extremely nervous about meeting Omar again. She couldn't help but think about being naked in his arms and warm and secure against his chest and now she had to fight those feelings to stop them rising to the surface again. She had to be professional and detached.

'Hello,' she said rather sheepishly as he finally came into the office. 'How is the film going?'

Omar didn't seem his usual full-of-life self.

'Not well—having to reshoot scenes, the budget's been blown and the producer's furious with it all. It's a shambles.'

'Oh,' Rani replied tentatively. She wanted to keep detached but show concern at the same time. 'That's a shame. Who's the producer?'

'I am!'

'Oh, I see, and do you have to tell yourself off?'

That brought half a smile to Omar's otherwise gloomy face.

'Anyway, I've got to get on,' Rani continued. 'Perhaps we can have an interview later or tomorrow—I need to ask you some questions and fill in some of the gaps.'

Omar looked quizzically at her as if he wasn't really paying attention, as if his mind was elsewhere. And it was.

'Yeah, sure, whatever, later. That'll be fine.'

They both turned away and went their separate ways.

Could have gone better, could have gone worse, Rani thought to herself.

Omar's mood hadn't improved when they sat down in one of the palatial living rooms later that evening to begin their first formal interview. He hadn't cooked, hadn't bothered changing and seemed agitated by something. Rani turned her recorder on and decided to press ahead. The book needed quotes and stories and they were only going to come from talking to Omar whatever mood he was in. It reminded her of their first encounter. It had been hard to get Omar to open up and be more than monosyllabic then. This time it seemed harder. He really was in no mood to open up and after about an hour Rani decided to call it off as a waste of time.

'Look, Omar, if you don't want to do this, then fine, we'll do it another time, but how do you expect me to write anything if you won't open up?' She waited for his response and when it came it was not what she'd expected.

'The studio has pulled the plug and shut the film down. They're not interested in it any more.'

Rani didn't immediately take on the significance of what Omar was saying.

'What does that mean? It's just a film—there will be others,' Rani suggested.

'No, there won't. It's a fickle industry and it only takes one flop or cock-up to end your career.' And Omar proceeded to list a plethora of famous actors whose careers had been sunk by costly, extravagant movies that hadn't been successful.

'But you don't have to work, do you? Just look at all of this.' And she pointed to the impressive paintings on the walls of the room they were sitting in and collections of exquisite china in their glass cabinets. 'It's not as if you need the money, is it?'

Omar let out an almighty laugh. It was so loud and demonic it made Rani jump with fright.

'That's exactly it!' he began. 'All of this, all of this has got to go. I'm finished, Rani, bankrupt!' he exclaimed.

Rani didn't understand and her face showed it.

'I haven't got a penny left, it's all gone, all gone into the movie, and now the bank wants its money back.'

'I don't understand. I thought the studio paid for everything.'

'They do, or rather they did,' Omar said, 'but they pulled out a month ago and since then I've been footing the bill for everything. Everything.'

'You mean all those people at the set I saw the other day—you're paying their wages?' The enormity of the situation sank in.

'Everything. The staff, the film, the cameras, the power and lighting bills, the catering, costumes and even the car-parking charges—everything!' Omar looked relieved to have let it all out. He took a deep breath and sighed. 'Tomorrow I'm going to have to shut the set down. It's over—it's all over.' He fell silent.

Rani looked across at him, the screen god of her youth, so powerful and strong, and here he was down and dejected.

'Worse things happen at sea,' she said awkwardly.

'What?'

'I said worse things happen at sea—that's the saying, isn't it? It's supposed to make you feel better!'

'Well, it didn't, I mean doesn't,' Omar replied sullenly. 'I borrowed the money from the bank hoping to finish the film off and I had to put the house up as collateral. Well, the movie isn't finished yet and the bank won't extend the loan any more so I've got no option.'

'Surely there's something you can do?'

'Nothing, I've mortgaged this place as well as my other properties, and there are art assessors coming in tomorrow to value all this stuff.'

Rani was hoping to find a ray of light among the gloom, something she could hold out to Omar to believe in.

'How much more do you need to film? What's the cost? Perhaps you could borrow money against the club?'

'Already done that.'

'What about advances from the book?' Rani said hopefully.

'Spent that as well—and you haven't even written it, yet!'

Rani was shocked.

'I told you it was all gone. Worst of all I've got to tell George I can't pay him. He even paid to fill the car on his way back from picking me up!' Omar struggled to push himself up from the sofa. His whole demeanour was of a worn-out man. The broad shoulders were sunken and curved inward and Rani noticed for the first time that he'd not shaved and in the stubble were flecks of white. Omar dragged himself off to bed and Rani was left alone with her thoughts. No sooner had she thought she'd straightened the confusion in her mind than along came another set of complications to stir it all up again. The cheek of the man to spend money from a book that wasn't written and wouldn't be unless he was prepared to give more of himself. At least a chapter on bank-rolling a failed movie and going bankrupt would guarantee some headlines and sell a few more copies, Rani thought, looking for something positive as she headed up to her own bedroom.

The next morning Rani was up early and headed straight to the office to begin working without stopping to make her customary pot of tea. Some time during the night she'd made up her mind to really get on with the book. Perhaps if she could deliver a rough draft of the first part to the publishers they'd release some more money to Omar. It was the only way she could think of helping him. She cared for him, whatever she told herself; even if he didn't feel the same way she couldn't turn her back on him. That day she busied herself in the book. Omar moped about the house and garden, wandering around the place with his mobile phone pinned to his ear. Each time he came within range Rani could hear the stress of the situation amplified in his voice.

The following evening Omar agreed to another interview. Rani set her recorder up again and produced a pot of tea from the kitchen. Before sitting down she went around the living room turning off all the lights.

'What are you doing? Omar asked.

'Saving you money,' Rani replied, lighting a couple of candles she'd put on the table between them. 'Anyway, candles make the place feel more cozy, don't they? Shall we get on with it?'

Omar was more open than before. He actually answered Rani's questions and several times even laughed about the things he had got up to with Digger when they were both young men in Manchester. He seemed a little more relaxed, even if occasionally he appeared to drift off somewhere else. When they'd finished talking he even smiled and thanked her. He was finding it hard to come to terms with his situation. He had been juggling the competing demands on his attention for too long and eventually he'd let them slip. Keeping the film afloat had been keeping him awake at night. Worrying about the finances had been occupying his waking moments and affecting his judgement at the set. He knew he was as much to blame as anyone for the delays but some things were out of his control and it was always at the moment of the greatest stress that another problem seemed to come along vying for attention and, invariably, money.

It was always about money. That was the way it seemed to Omar. As a small boy he could remember his father being obsessed with making, borrowing or begging enough money to make his deals and blow on ludicrous business ventures. In Pakistan people struggled to make enough to feed themselves and their families. Now the accountants were calling time on the movie because there wasn't enough money to keep it going. He was so close to finishing and now the studio had pulled out they'd left him with the footage. If only he could scrape together enough to edit it he was certain it would be an excellent film. As he wandered aimlessly around the mansion he afforded himself a smile as he thought how ironic his situation was. He had believed he was untouchable once he'd made his fortune, that his name was enough to get things done, and here he was, broke. Right back where he started and having to sell his privacy to keep the wolves from the door, selling his own story while at the same time criticising his father for doing the very same.

Everyone had wanted to be his friend when he was wealthy—the businessmen, and studio executives who threw money at him when he didn't need or want it. The women who had leapt at the chance to be with him because of his fame and fortune. But it was all gone or going and he only had his own vanity to blame. He'd thought he could control his destiny but in reality he was finding out that he couldn't. The only thing left was to sell himself and he even had to rely upon someone else to help him do that.

Over the next few days Rani buried herself in her work. She didn't venture out of the office except to sleep and eat. She had become engrossed in the process. Occasionally Omar would creep up to the door and watch her silently without disturbing her. He said nothing, not wanting to betray his presence. He knew he was taking comfort in her being around.

'I've made you breakfast,' Omar said, knocking on the door of Rani's room. 'Can I bring it in?' He hovered nervously outside waiting for a reply.

Still half asleep, Rani replied without thinking. Omar carried the tray into her room and placed it on the sideboard.

'There's orange juice, toast and scrambled eggs, my own special recipe, some fruit salad and, of course, a large pot of tea,' he exclaimed.

He made a point of looking away from the bed, not wanting to be caught looking at her, but at the same time curious to see what she looked like. It was the first time they had been so intimate since they had spent the night together and both of them were fully aware of it. Omar addressed the bedroom in general as he described the sort of day it was outside and he drew back the curtains to show Rani.

'You see, it looks like it's going to be a sunny one. Perhaps you'd like to go for a walk a little later, if you're not too busy?'

'I'm a little tied up with work at the moment; you see, I've got this demanding boss!' Rani replied.

'Ah, yes, of course,' Omar said, 'but maybe we

should have a look around the gardens before the bailiffs move in!'

They smiled at each other. It was the first time they had shared a joke in weeks. Rani felt the telltale signs of a racing pulse and quickly diverted the conversation back onto safer ground.

'Well, whatever you think best,' Omar said as he left the room. 'You know where I am if you want me.' He withdrew rather reluctantly.

For the first time since she'd returned Rani walked into the kitchen after a morning's work knowing she would probably bump into Omar. Sure enough he was there and he was cooking for the first time in days.

'Aloo baingan with lemon chicken and rice—how does that sound?'

'Tasty,' Rani replied as she moved towards the bubbling pots to cast her eye over the preparation.

'Here—try some,' Omar said, taking a small spoon out of the drawer and offering a little taster to Rani's lips.

She tentatively opened them as he blew gently on the spoon. Rani made a note of his consideration as she let him put the spoon into her mouth and closed her lips around it. The aloo baingan tasted exquisite and she felt her knees almost buckle at the sensations exploding in her mouth. Omar was excited by Rani's reaction and his face lit up for the first time in a long time. It felt right being with her, being this close.

'I'm going away for a few days tomorrow. It's my mother's birthday and I never miss visiting,' Rani said with a trembling voice. The light that had flickered on Omar's face blinked and vanished. Rani saw the happiness dim and heard a hint of regret in Omar's reply.

'Oh, OK' was all he could say.

'I'll be back,' she said. 'We've a book to finish, haven't we?'

The next morning Omar watched from the library window as George drove Rani to the station. She wasn't like any of the others, he thought to himself. He had been wrong to even think it. He continued to stare out across the gardens until the car disappeared from view and there was no longer anything to keep his gaze. He found his thoughts wandering as he made his way downstairs and into the great hall. There were packing cases already assembled ready to receive the collections of fine china and glass. He smiled to himself as he walked past the fragile objects. He'd never really understood them; he knew he'd only bought them to show off and he didn't have any attachment to them. They were just symbols, outward signs to show how successful he had been. Success measured by money, conspicuously displayed for other people's benefit, and of course to show off! But as he made his way towards the cinema and the editing room he knew he wouldn't miss them; they were just baubles and he was better off without them. Rani, on the other hand, was something else. She had really got her teeth into the book. She was enjoying it and he was enjoying that experience. She had brought some light into the darkness of his financial troubles and it had nothing to do with the money he was getting from it. That was already owed to the banks. She had come back to him after he'd dismissed her concerns about his marriage.

Marriage—that was a fine word to use for such an arrangement! He'd only met his 'bride' on the day of the wedding forced on him by a bullying father. Afterwards she only spent a month living with him in his father's shabby apartment in Lahore before fleeing back to her family. What concern was it of his? He had only been seventeen and didn't love her—how could he? It wasn't possible to force yourself into love and he'd had no intention of sleeping with her and playing happy families—his father couldn't make him do that. So she'd left. His father had taken the money Omar's wife had brought as a dowry to the marriage and Omar had left to make his own fortune, determined to prevent his father from making money out of him ever again.

It all seemed so different with Rani. He'd misjudged her from the outset. *She didn't even let me touch her bottom when we were dancing!* Omar thought to himself. There weren't any women he'd met since he'd become so famous that had denied him that pleasure! He enjoyed the recollection of that evening. She really could dance well and had looked devastatingly attractive. The revolving door that they'd both met in had spun her back towards him once more and Omar knew that he wasn't going to let her out of his reach again.

CHAPTER TEN

RANI WAS DELIGHTED to be back with her parents for a while. Being with an intense Omar for so long had been tiring. The book was going really well and the feedback from the publishers to her first chapters had been remarkable. She had managed to avoid spending too much time alone with Omar and was impressed with herself for not thinking about him more than fifty times a day. She had got back on the horse and was learning to ride again.

As a birthday treat for her mother Rani always took her out shopping for a day. They headed for the Belgrave Road in Leicester, the famous Golden Mile. There was nowhere outside India that offered such a wide range of jewellery shops, sari houses and material stalls. Rani drove them and played her mother's favourite Mohammed Rafi tracks all the way there.

'You know, Rani, he really could sing. What a voice. Oh, I was so sad when he passed on.'

They sang along together to 'Aaj Mausam Bada Beiman Hai' and memories of growing up in India came flooding back for Rani's mother.

Leicester was buzzing. There were hundreds of mothers and daughters doing just what they were doing. Walking slowly along the pavement in front of the shops with their eyes fixed firmly on the displays of beautiful clothes. They stopped to admire the jewellery in one store and they took it in turns to try on pieces.

'I'll take it,' Mrs de Silver said to the owner of one shop as she slid a glass bracelet from her wrist.

'Let me buy that for you, Mummy,' Rani said.

'No, no. You can't.'

'Why not? It's your birthday. Let me.'

'How can I, Rani? It's for you!' her mother said with delight as she handed it to her daughter. Rani hugged her mother and insisted on buying her halwa puri, the deep-fried chapatti served with aromatic, spicy chick-peas and potato. As an extra treat they bought fresh jalebi from the men making it on the street.

'You know, this reminds me so much of India. Your father would die if he knew I was eating from a street vendor!' Mrs de Silver said. 'He'd be asking the fellow if he'd washed his hands!' They smiled as they crunched through the sugary coating of the jalebi into the gooey fried centre.

'Now I know why these things are so bad for you,' Mrs de Silver said.

'Yes, because they taste so good!' Rani replied. 'You just want to eat more!'

Her father never accompanied them. He didn't like shopping; he didn't like crowds and he could never understand why it took his wife and daughter so long to buy the simplest of things like clothes. Why did they have to try everything in the shop on and in every conceivable combination before they actually made a purchase? Mrs de Silver bought all his clothes for him.

Dr de Silver was waiting for them at the front door when they returned from their shopping expedition.

'Where have you been?' he said in an agitated voice.

'You know perfectly well where we've been, Daddy ji. Why? What's all the commotion? Have you been waiting for someone to make you a cup of tea?' Rani replied cheekily and handed him a box of matai.

'We didn't forget you, did we? We've got your favourite, ladoo.'

Her mother laughed.

'Yes, what's all the fuss, Pappa?'

Dr de Silver walked back into the house.

'What the hell is going on here?' he said, pointing at the dozens of bunches of flowers in the hall. Rani and her mother walked in, bemused. Their sweets were not the only gifts in the house. There were more bouquets in the living room and in the kitchen. Roses, lilies and carnations. Large sprays of exotic red-hot pokers with their red and yellow florets, gypsophila in all colours, primulas tied up with raffia, whole bowls of exquisite living orchids in bright and exotic colours. There were flowers of all kinds on every other surface.

'So, Rani, can you explain all this?' her father asked.

Mrs de Silver had already begun reading some of the little notes tied or tucked into the flowers. They all had short messages on them, just a few words but all along the same theme. Some of them were handwritten and signed Omar.

'They're all from him!' Mrs de Silver said to her husband.

'Exactly,' he replied. 'Well, Rani, what does it all mean?'

Rani wasn't sure what it meant. She looked at the notes. They were short and to the point. *I'm sorry. I miss you. I need you.*

'So he's been sending you flowers, is it, this man you are working for?'

'It looks that way, Daddy!'

'Urm,' grumbled her protective father. 'And what is he trying to say with all these blooms? That's what they say about flowers isn't it—say it with flowers? Well, he's obviously got a lot to say! Any of it sensible? You know, I came to this country with just ten pounds, just ten, yes, that's right, not quite enough to buy one of your harlot-coloured lipsticks, I bet, eh!'

Rani smiled at her father's description of the bright colours she wore for make-up and the value judgement he loaded onto them, but mostly because he really had no idea how much they cost.

'Ten pounds in my pocket and the address of your uncle Rashid, that's all I had. Now your mother will tell you how we struggled.' He looked across to his wife, who was trying to remain neutrally positioned between daughter and husband. Both had heard the story a hundred times but that wouldn't stop Dr de Silver repeating one more time for good measure.

'And you know what I did with that ten pounds?'

'Yes, Daddy, you bought some chickens and started your own egg business.'

'I bought some chickens and started my own egg business.' His sentence overlapped Rani's as he continued to talk, oblivious to her response.

'And with that money I put myself through medical school, that's right, paid for it all myself, the tuition, the equipment and I even bought a flat, all from that ten pounds and those chickens. And this is how you choose to repay your mother and me, is it, hanging out in nightclubs and discotheques, with actors?'

Rani smiled again as the word 'discotheque' left her father's lips.

'Oh, Dad, nobody calls them discotheques any more, not since the seventies!'

'Well, whatever they are called, they are dark places filled with the lowest form of people, cavorting and gyrating and getting up to all sorts.'

Now his wife smiled at him as well.

'Pappa, they are just young people having fun, remember, fun.' She looked at him with eyes that said, *You've already said enough, now leave it to me.* He didn't realise, so she continued to stare and added, 'Remember St Barts Christmas Party, 1973?'

That was all she needed to say to shut Dr de Silver up. He went quiet and walked down towards the large patio windows that overlooked the rear of the house. He was the sort of man who was extremely certain in himself and his own judgement. He knew what it was like to struggle; he knew the sacrifices required to give his only child everything he had hankered after as a young man. He stared through the window towards the flower beds and swimming pool, the elegant ornamental gazebo and the large, two-storey Wendy house he'd built for Rani.

'Pappa, she is growing up,' his wife said as she joined him at the window. She knew he was thinking about the long summer days when they had played with Rani the toddler in paddling pools and run around the garden laughing and giggling as she'd chased butterflies and bees.

'It seems like just last week, doesn't it?' she said, smiling at him. He nodded. His wife had always been able to read his mind. 'But it is not. She is a young woman, she has the needs of a young woman, so the least we can do is listen to her.' She paused and waited for him to make some sort of acceptance. He grunted and turned back to Rani, sighing heavily.

'So what is this man, eh?' He didn't wait for a response, preferring to give his own answers. 'I'll tell you what he is, a gutter-born, jumped-up, fly-by-night entertainer. Not a proper job. So why all the flowers? Is he feeling so guilty, he needs just a cheap gimmick to impress you, the sort of thing men like that pull?' stated Dr de Silver with confidence in his own ability to judge others. 'All show and no substance, I told you, he's only after one thing and this is his way of trying to get it.'

Mrs de Silver had made her way into the conservatory at the back of the house, following the trail of flowers. She let out a gasp.

'What is it, Mummy?'

'Come and take a look, Rani. You won't believe your eyes.'

'Oh, my God.'

There was a collection of teddy bears, cute-looking rabbits, and fluffy sheep.

'Are those real?' Rani asked, pointing at a string of pearls hanging round the neck of a wide-eyed bear.

Mrs de Silver nodded.

'I think so,' she said calmly.

'And what about these?' Rani said, holding up a stuffed pig sporting a large diamond necklace and earrings.

'I guess so.'

'Gimmicks!' Dr de Silver said as he joined them. His wife continued to look through the mound of toys, gasping as she came across more expensive-looking jewellery hanging from them.

'You could try sending me a few *gimmicks* like these from time to time,' she said under her breath.

But their investigation was interrupted by the noise coming from the road outside their house. Dr de Silver was annoyed his rant had been disturbed by the growing din. Rani was relieved. She ran to see what the cause of all the racket was. Her eyes almost popped from their sockets as the sound became a vision as well. A dozen dohl players were making their way along the middle of the road, banging their drums for all they were worth. It was like the sound of thunder rolling towards them. The men were all wearing bright white turbans and scarlet waistcoats with baggy white trousers and gold Aladdin shoes.

'What on earth is going on now?' Dr de Silver exclaimed as he joined Rani at the window.

'I don't know, Abu ji,' Rani said softly, hoping to placate her father's anger by allowing him the space to complain about something else. Deep inside she had the feeling she knew exactly what was going on and as the drummers stopped directly outside her parents' house her suspicions were realised.

'Oh hell, he's on an elephant!' her father exclaimed.

Sure enough, riding high in the wooden box seat on the back of an impressive-looking bull elephant was Omar. An elaborate multicoloured canopy over his head was the final touch.

'Calm yourself, dear,' his wife said as she placed a restraining hand on his forearm. 'Remember what your doctor said.' That was enough to send her husband off into another diatribe.

'My doctor! I was his tutor, he was my student, I got him his degree and now he has the cheek to lecture me about my high blood pressure! What do you expect with a wayward daughter cavorting with unsavoury film wallah like this idiot?' He was almost foaming at the mouth as he gestured towards Omar and his entourage. The shame he felt about his daughter's relationship was nothing to the embarrassment that suddenly stuck him when he thought about all of his friends and neighbours in their exclusive road. Sure enough as he looked from his window at the carnival scene that had made camp on his expansive gravel drive he also saw the familiar faces of his neighbours.

'Oh, my God!' he said as his head dropped into his cupped hands. 'They are all out there. Look at them!' He was right: dozens of his neighbours had gathered to witness the spectacle. There would be no living this down at the golf club or at his practice. The drumming didn't stop either—there was no way the caravan was going to be moved until Omar had been listened to.

Rani had scurried upstairs to the front bedroom of the house for a better look. Her heart had found its lost beat and she could feel it thumping away beneath her breasts as it had the first time she'd seen him. She had a sudden naughty memory of them in bed together and it felt warm and exciting.

She pushed her face to the glass, taking in the latest and the greatest of Omar's overt declarations of his feelings. He obviously sensed she was watching and looked up. Their eyes met.

'Rani, Rani,' her father bellowed up the wide staircase. 'Come down here, come on, beti!'

She bounded down the stairs and met her parents in the hall.

'Right, let's sort this out once and for all,' Dr de Silver said and marched them all out of the house. There were cheers and applause from the surrounding crowd. Some now had their video cameras and phones out filming the whole thing. Dr de Silver tried to look as dignified as possible, as if having a circus parked on his front lawn were an everyday event.

'My God, he looks like Hannibal! And what is that elephant doing to my lawn?'

The elephant was doing what large elephants did and was providing enough manure to supply a rose garden for a year.

Omar swung down from the back of his mount and landed at the feet of Mrs de Silver, who couldn't help herself when they came face to face.

'Ooh, your eyes are even greener than in the films.' She gasped, which earned her a withering look from her husband and an embarrassed sigh from her daughter. But her reaction to Omar's over-the-top display was at least positive. Rani knew that when he began talking to her mother he would have her eating out of his hand in a few minutes. Her father was a tougher prospect.

'Rani, I must talk to you,' Omar said from beneath his white-feathered turban.

Rani stood with her hands behind her back like a coy schoolgirl standing in front of the captain of the first fifteen.

'Whatever it is you have to say to my daughter you can say in front of me!' Dr de Silver put himself between his daughter and Omar and puffed out his chest.

Omar shrugged his shoulders and began.

'Thank you, Rani. I've heard from the publishers. They've told me all about your fabulous chapters. They already think they'll be printing a million copies in the first run! It's amazing. You're amazing! You know I wasn't born with a silver spoon in my mouth. We were lucky enough to have food for ours and sometimes we went without. I've struggled to get where I am. Fought hard for what's mine while you've sat back and let Daddy do everything for you.'

Rani looked on as Omar's face grew redder. She was frightened. Frightened what he might do, frightened that what he was saying about her was the truth. She had had it easy and been supported all the way by her family. Her father looked embarrassed at being dragged into the conversation. Omar noticed his unease and turned to him with his hands together as in prayer.

'Forgive me, I didn't mean to insult you, sir, but when you come from my part of town you've got to do it for yourself or go without. There aren't any helping hands or trust funds. And no one to smooth the way.' He paused, looking back towards Rani. 'Well, I didn't think there was anyone to help. I really didn't think there was anyone who really cared about me and I was wrong. So very wrong on that score. I don't ever want to be without you again. Can you forgive me?' Rani could feel the burning heat of her love for Omar growing inside.

'But what about that old paperwork?' she said, referring to his marriage certificate she had uncovered in his office.

Her parents looked on, not understanding the reference.

'Well, that's another reason I'm here; they say bad things happen in threes, don't they? Well, so does good luck!' Omar quickly began to explain about how things had been resolved.

'You know things had got bad, with money and the film was under threat and everything? Well, one of the paintings I bought many years ago when I first became famous has just auctioned for a fortune!'

'So he's had to sell his belongings to make ends

meet!' exclaimed Dr de Silver throwing up his hands. 'Why am I not surprised?'

'Oh, Daddy, do be quiet!' Rani said forcefully. 'Let him explain!'

Everyone looked at Rani with a sense of stunned shock. But her interruption did the trick. Her father didn't say another word while Omar continued his story.

'I used some of the money to finish the film and, as I thought it would, it's turned out really well, advance sales are far, far better than expected and it's set to break opening day records across India and over here.'

Rani's father was visibly relieved by the news that Omar was solvent again.

'And the other thing?' Rani asked tentatively.

'That's the best news. I got my lawyer to hire some private detectives and they've been working on it ever since that day, you know?'

Rani nodded, understanding Omar was talking about the day at his house when she had confronted him with his marriage paperwork. In that moment, outside her parents' home, she realised he did care, that he had been trying to unravel the problems of his past. That he wanted to make things right for her, for them.

Rani held back, wanting to be absolutely sure that Omar was as good as his word.

'Honestly?' She looked deep into his eyes as she asked him.

'Honestly,' he replied. 'My lawyer told me this morning—it's all been sorted. Because of a lack of witnesses it was never legal in the first place. It seems my father had bribed the official who had signed the document.'

Rani's parents looked on, bemused and confused by what was being said, but even her father didn't interrupt.

'Rani, she never was...I mean we never were—!' Just as Omar was about to say the word 'married' Rani put a finger to her lips to stop him; she didn't want to hear him use it unless it was about them. She could tell by his expression that he was telling the truth and her relief was total. Her face lit up for the first time in weeks, as if the very essence of life had returned to her.

'Let's go inside,' suggested Mrs de Silver. 'We've given the neighbours plenty to gossip about already.'

Inside the house Omar slipped off his shoes as Rani took him by the hand and began showing him around. She felt light and airy inside, as if all the pressure and weight had been lifted. The anxious knots in her stomach had begun to unravel and every moment she touched Omar's skin she felt more complete.

'Here's a picture of Daddy and the High Commissioner—they went to the same university,' Rani said, loud enough to ensure her father could hear the fuss she was making about him. She knew he was won over by the revelation about Omar's hard-won success and his financial security, but she just wanted to make sure with some well-placed flattery.

'I'm just going to show Omar the upstairs,' Rani called out as she began climbing the wide central staircase.

'Don't be too long. I'm making tea,' her mother replied.

'Come on, quickly, I've something to show you,' Rani said eagerly. Her heart was racing faster and faster and she could feel the excitement building. 'This way—it's my old bedroom,' she added with a naughty smile.

'Wait there, and close your eyes,' she ordered as they reached the door.

A few moments later she called him in.

'You can come in now, but keep your eyes closed.'

Omar stepped cautiously through the open doorway and into the room. It was relatively large and just like any teenage girl's room. There was a dressing table with photographs of her parents and other family members. There were pots of hairbrushes and an assortment of sprays and perfume bottles. On the bed was a collection of obviously well-loved soft toys.

'What did you want to show me?' Omar asked with his eyes still firmly shut.

'Open your eyes!' Rani said.

On the wall was a rather worn-looking poster. It was a promotional one, for Omar's film, *Sacred Heart.*

'You see, I really have been a fan of yours for quite some time!' Rani said, pointing at the poster. There was a large red heart drawn on it and inside the initials *'O and R for ever'* written. Rani blushed.

'So I see!' Now it was Omar's turn to get embarrassed. 'For ever,' he repeated what he was reading. 'And you think we can, you know, red heart for ever?'

Rani walked towards the star of the poster that now stood life-size and one hundred per cent real in her bedroom and stood on tiptoe to kiss him. Omar bent down to meet her lips and they locked themselves together. Omar's hands began to slide expertly down Rani's body. Oh, how he really wanted her now; this was the moment. Rani was desperate to oblige and melted in his arms. But it was wrong. They couldn't, not there, not in her parents' house. She was overcome with lust and guilt all at once. Rani could already feel herself getting excited. Omar was wide-eyed and instantly on fire. This time it was Rani who had to pull away from the magnetism of the moment, to break them apart before things went too far.

'We can't,' she whispered. 'Not here, not now, it isn't—'

'I know,' Omar reluctantly accepted, 'but—' he began again.

Rani interrupted him.

'No buts. I am yours, will be yours for ever, just like I dreamed of. So do you like my room?'

'I love what's in it,' Omar replied.

'You do say the nicest things,' Rani said, 'and they always make me blush! But I've something else for you.' And her tone changed. Her face became more serious.

Omar looked perturbed.

'What is it?'

Rani was hesitant and began rather nervously.

'I know you never knew her—your mother, that is.' And she pulled an envelope from the bedside cabinet and passed it to Omar. 'I've been doing some detective work of my own, and this is what I've found.'

Now it was Omar's turn to be shocked and hesitant. He took the envelope reluctantly; his hands were shaking. Rani noticed and held them.

'I'm really sorry,' she said as tears began to water in her eyes. 'She's…'

'Dead,' Omar continued. 'I always knew she was—well, always felt she was,' he corrected himself.

Now Rani squeezed both his hands.

'But she didn't abandon you, no matter what your father told you. She never left you, never walked out on you.'

Omar looked to Rani for the answer.

'Omar, she died giving birth to you. It seems there were complications, things went wrong and the doctors couldn't save her. I'm so sorry.' She threw her arms around his chest and clung on for dear life.

Omar sniffed. He was trying to prevent the emotion he felt from betraying him as tears. His arms closed around Rani, around the woman who loved him, whom he loved more than anything in the world.

'I've found out all I can. It's in the envelope. You don't have to read it, not now—whenever, just when you feel you can. But I've even managed to find an old school report; she was quite a cook, your mum, according to what the teachers wrote. Perhaps that's where you get it from!'

Omar sniffed again. He knew Rani loved him. Why else would she go to all this trouble if not for love?

'She didn't leave you. Know that, my darling,' Rani said as he squeezed her tighter. 'She would never have done that. She wasn't that sort of woman.'

George pulled up in the stretched Mercedes and stepped out. He walked smartly up to the front door and was greeted by Rani.

'Hello, George. It's nice to see you again.'

'Good afternoon, Miss Rani. May I say how nice it is to see you? Is Mr Khan with you?'

Omar put his head out of the door.

'I'll be with you in a moment, George.' And he turned back into the house to say goodbye to Rani's parents, who followed the couple out of the house and down to the waiting car.

'Would you care to get inside, miss?' George asked as he opened the rear door.

Rani looked around at her parents. She no longer felt guilty.

'What about these elephants?' Dr de Silver shouted as the car pulled away.

'Keep them!' Omar called back. 'They'll be good for the garden!'

Rani's flabbergasted parents watched open-mouthed as their only daughter disappeared out of view and they were left with a circus act to clear up.

'What are you staring at?' Dr de Silver addressed his neighbours, who were just as bewildered by the whole display as he was. 'So, we have elephants!'

'Where are you taking me?' Rani asked.

The car stopped abruptly as George pulled into the kerb.

'What are you doing?' Omar asked.

'She's got a point, boss. Where are we going? You've not told me yet and anyway I'm not driving another inch unless you two sort things out.'

Rani and Omar looked quizzically at each other and then at George.

'I've seen the pair of you. Don't think I haven't. He's been going around with a face longer than a wet weekend and you, Miss Rani, well, I'm sure I saw how you felt the moment you first stepped into our lives. You're made for each other and if—'

'George—' Omar tried to stop him.

'No, let me say my piece. Fire me if you like, but I'll say it nevertheless.'

'But, George—' This time it was Rani trying to interrupt him.

'With respect, Miss Rani, I've started so I'll finish. Just hear me out, please. You're like two spoilt children who've got everything but won't share with one another. You can't let go of your heart for fear of losing it to a woman who you think is superior to you,' he said, looking directly at Omar, 'and you can't imagine falling in love with someone you see as below you so you won't let go either. You are scared of the same thing—letting go…' he paused for breath '…but if you don't let go of the things holding you back you'll never be able to hold onto each other and you'll lose everything. So kiss and makeup, get it sorted or I'm getting out of the car. There, that's it. Now you can fire me!' George said and turned back to face the road.

Omar and Rani looked at each other in a state of shock. They had just received relationship advice from their driver and were stunned.

'You know, George, you're right. That's why we've already kissed and made up,' said Omar, 'but we'll kiss again if it will make you happy.'

Rani leant in towards Omar. His head tilted down to meet hers.

'I think we should try making up more often,' Rani said as his lips found hers and they kissed. George started going red as he looked up into his rear-view mirror and the car began to slowly pull away from the kerb.

'Where to, sir?' he asked as confidently as he could, trying to pretend he'd never said what he'd just said.

'Shambles.'

'Very good, Mr Khan.' And George set off towards the exclusive restaurant beside the Thames at Richmond.

From the front, the restaurant had the appearance of a tidy-looking house with an expanse of well-kept lawn and mature trees. George drove past it and turned down a narrow alley at the side into a deceptively large car park. The rear of the building ran down on terraces towards the banks of the Thames. Diners seated on this side had an excellent view across the lawns and flower borders towards Eel Pie Island in the middle of the river.

'Wow! What a fantastic-looking place,' Rani said as they walked beneath a large arbour, heavy with rose blossom, up towards the entrance. 'I never knew it existed and I must have been passed it hundreds of times.'

'That's one of its attractions. No signs, no reviews in the papers, just word-of-mouth recommendation,' Omar said. He realised he was about to show off again and stopped himself from saying any more. They were met by the maître d'.

'Good afternoon, Mr Khan, Miss de Silver, so nice to have you with us.'

Rani looked at Omar.

'How did he know my name?'

Omar shrugged his shoulders and smiled. Their table was next to the large windows and offered them the prime view.

'Some bubbles, please, Raymond.'

'Very good, Mr Khan.'

He returned almost immediately with a large champagne cooler and a bottle of wine.

'I took the liberty of putting it on ice when you called with your reservation.'

Rani looked at Omar with the same quizzical stare.

'A bit presumptuous of you,' she said. 'How did you know I'd agree to get in the car with you?'

'I didn't, but any boy scout knows that it's best to be prepared!'

Omar's face turned from smile to serious as he leant in towards Rani.

'You know what George said, back in the car? He's right. We are very similar. Strong-willed.'

'Stubborn?' Rani suggested.

'That too, and both weighed down with the baggage of our pasts. Yes, there have been other women in my life; at my age do you think it would be any different? But there's never been a you in my life, not someone who can make the passion rise from love to hatred and everything in between. You drive me wild and have me pulling at my hair with frustration with your polite manners and correct pronunciation but I love it. I love you. My cards are on the table in front of you!' Omar announced, but Rani sat motionless. Omar quickly stood up and addressed the entire room.

'Ladies and gentlemen, I would like you all to know that I believe my dining companion is the most exquisite creature I have ever known, the most perfect form my eyes have ever looked upon and I have fallen in love with her!' He raised his glass in salute and sat down to a polite round of applause from the other guests. Rani stared dumbfounded, unable to speak. She had never been spoken of in those terms before and in such a public way.

'The moment I saw you I knew you were the right woman for me. I just couldn't let myself go,' Omar said. 'And when I read what you wrote about me in your article, I hoped you truly felt the same way as the words you used.' He paused, waiting for a response. Not getting one, he continued anxiously, 'Perhaps I was wrong.'

'No, no, you're not wrong, I just, well, I mean to say…' Rani stumbled over every word she was trying to pronounce '…what I didn't realise was just, oh, what do I mean to say?' She stopped and took a sip from the glass in front of her, took a deep breath and began again.

'I've never felt this way before. I was shocked by my reaction to meeting you. You triggered something inside me that I didn't know was there. Does that sound silly?' Omar shook his head and rested his chin on his hand.

'I mean, I don't believe in love at first sight. I'm not

that daft! Well, that's how I felt, and now I've stupidly gone and told the whole world!' Rani sighed.

'You know, I too would never have thought love at first sight was possible, but I do believe in kismet. Some things are destined to be. When, where or what we can't tell, not until it happens, of course—' Omar took Rani's hands in his '—but I felt the same thing as you: kismet.' He leant across the table and kissed Rani full on her lips. His caress was gentle but it still sent a shock wave from her lips that flooded every part of her body.

'Why didn't you say something then? When we met?' Rani asked. 'Or even after I stayed with you? Why didn't you say something after I wrote that article about you in the papers?'

Omar looked thoughtful.

'Because I was scared and afraid. Women try it on all the time with me,' he said, and, seeing Rani's reaction, he added, 'so it's not unusual for pretty ones to attach themselves to me, for their benefit. So I've grown more selfish, more inward-looking, more defensive of my life.'

'And you thought I was one of those women?'

'Truthfully?'

Rani nodded.

'Well, yes, I thought so, but, before you get angry again, I still wanted you. After all, I made the first move, didn't I?'

Rani looked puzzled.

'It was me that asked you to write the book, wasn't it?'

'Yes, I suppose so,' she said slowly. 'Why did you agree to me writing it, anyway?'

'Ah, now you have me. That was selfish too.' And for the first time Rani watched as Omar squirmed in his seat. 'I needed someone to write it, you came along to interview me and you were like a little angel, an answer to my prayers, and very good-looking as well! I thought I could spend time with you in my life—that's what I honestly thought.'

'I was an opportunity, then!' Rani was still a little put out by his past attitude towards her.

Omar took Rani's hands and began to rub her fingers with his thumbs, playing with them.

'Perhaps, at first, but you know when you told me to go to hell you woke me up, as if I had been sleepwalking and didn't know where I was going. You made me look inside myself. You're the only woman who has done that. And you came back—you came back to help me, didn't you?'

Rani smiled.

'I know I was miserable, I know how I behaved, and I certainly wasn't happy that you made me feel that way.'

'I made you feel that way?'

'Yes,' he said.

'Then, what are we doing here? Why should we be together at all?'

'Because the anger I felt inside myself was from my own frustration. I mistook you, I didn't value you as I should have and I was annoyed with you for making me feel that way. I know now that frustration comes from love and it's because you love that other person that you get so angry, especially when they tell you something about yourself that's right! Something that you can't admit to yourself.'

Rani was stunned by Omar's interpretation of her feelings but he was right. Honesty hurt, and honesty when it came from someone you loved hurt even more.

'Love, you said love.'

'I did, because I do—I love you.'

'You've never said that to a woman before?'

'No, because I wouldn't say it, especially to you, without meaning it.'

'How can I be sure? You once told me you had said it and not meant it.'

'You have a good memory, Rani, but I think I also said that was because I had said it as an actor. But I'm not acting now. I don't need to with you. I can be myself at last.'

'And what can I be?'

Omar produced a small, exquisitely carved wooden box from inside his tunic and placed it on the table, opening it to face Rani. She gasped as the lid lifted to reveal its contents.

'You can be anything you want to be. But how about being my wife?'

Rani was mesmerised by the ring. It was the most brilliant blue sapphire set in a band of platinum. She was speechless.

'Right, shall we eat?' Omar said, slightly uncomfortable with the intensity of the moment and worried he'd proposed too soon.

'Yes,' Rani uttered through barely open lips.

'Yes, what? Yes, let's eat or yes, you'll be my wife?'

'Yes, yes, yes, to both!' Rani's eyes lit up and the sparkle and smile that Omar had first spotted exploded from her face. 'Yes, I'll be your wife and I'm starving! What's the soup of the day?' Rani asked.

'Pea,' said the waiter. Rani and Omar fell about laughing as the bewildered waiter looked on nervously.

'We'll have a bowl of soup, then,' Omar said.

'And two spoons,' added Rani, looking into the sparkling green eyes of her husband-to-be.

EPILOGUE

RANI HAD NEVER wanted an extravagant wedding. But she wasn't going to be allowed to get away with a few friends at the local register office. For one thing she was marrying Bollywood royalty and for that reason alone things were going to be on a grand scale. If Omar's film had flopped at the cinema perhaps they might have been able to get away with a more modest event, a few hundred guests, a sprinkling of celebrities and an elephant or two. But his film was a massive hit, playing in thousands of cinemas worldwide, even in America, where negotiations for the rights to make a film about his life story were well advanced. He was propelled back to the top of the A-list and, because he had bought the rights to the movie when the studio pulled the plug, he alone made all the money. The publication of Rani's book was fuel to the fire. The revelations it contained made headlines right around the world. Everyone wanted to see and be seen with Omar Khan, the Lion of Bollywood, and the woman who had tamed him. They were dubbed the *'Silver Screen Dream Team'*, the hottest property on the planet. So even by Bollywood standards Rani's big day was a phenomenon the like of which had never been seen before. And then there were her mother and father. Although he couldn't afford to pay for the occasion, Dr de Silver wanted things to be done properly and Omar agreed. It became a Western fusion of a traditional Hindu ceremony and opening night party. They hired the imposing Chatsworth House in Derbyshire, home of a real life duke and duchess and film set for various movies. Set in a thousand acres of beautifully landscaped and managed parkland, the house was fitting for the Bollywood wedding of the decade. Rani's mother along with Sunita and Shilpa organised a sangeet a week before the big day, and because Omar didn't have any family he wanted to be there George, his driver, and Digger, his one-time school friend, were roped in, much to their embarrassment.

'I don't understand a word they're saying,' George proclaimed to Rani over the noise of the women singing traditional songs to the sound of the dholki.

The sangeet was followed by the mehendi when all of Rani's friends were covered in wonderfully ornate henna designs. She enjoyed the attention and it fuelled her excitement and expectation for the wedding day itself. Omar arrived at Chatsworth in a gold helicopter, flying in from his own country house. An intricate floral design was created on the helicopter landing pad, made from thousands and thousands of orange and yellow marigolds. They were whisked into the air by the rotor blades and floated back down over the guests as a vibrant gentle coloured rain. Omar leapt from the helicopter wearing a long flowing white and gold suit, studded with pearls and jewels. He looked every inch the film star who had dominated Bollywood for so many years. A hundred dhol players accompanied him as he walked towards Dr and Mrs de Silver. It sounded like rolling thunder and shook the ground. He bowed gracefully and Rani's mother marked his forehead with a red bindi.

They made their way towards the house past huge floral displays fifteen feet high. They towered over the gardens made with more marigolds, brilliantly vivid purple and pink orchids, fragrant jasmine and red roses of every shade from pale pink to deep blood red. The entire front of the house was bathed in strings of sparkling white lights hung from the roof to the ground; they created the illusion of a cascading waterfall.

As Omar saw Rani for the first time that day he thought she looked more beautiful than ever before. She wore a traditional red sari edged with gold and decorated with exquisite embroidery. Pearls and jewels to match his own suit and complement Rani's exquisitely crafted panjangla were sewn into the fine fabric.

They exchanged garlands of colourful flowers before starting the series of sacraments that would bond them together as husband and wife. The ceremony, with all its intricate rituals, lasted for hours but for Rani and Omar it seemed like only minutes. They were so transfixed by each other that they didn't break eye contact for the entire day. And keeping an eye on them was a giant statue of Ganesh decorated with flowers and surrounded with offerings of matai and ludoo, ever vigilant, watching as they set out on a new path together. As they kissed for the first time in front of the hundreds of guests a cheer and spontaneous applause rose from the onlookers. Sunita and Shilpa hugged each other, George squeezed his wife's hand and Rani's parents sobbed uncontrollably. They hadn't lost a daughter; they'd gained a son-in-law.

Omar leant forward and whispered in her ear, 'Mira shoneya, I love you so very much. You have captured my heart.' A tear welled in his eyes as he spoke and Rani blinked rapidly and turned away so Omar couldn't see her cry with joy.

'And I love you too, Omar,' she replied, dabbing her eye on the hem of her sari. 'You are my silver-screen dream come true.'

* * * * *

Mills & Boon® Hardback

April 2013

ROMANCE

Master of her Virtue	Miranda Lee
The Cost of her Innocence	Jacqueline Baird
A Taste of the Forbidden	Carole Mortimer
Count Valieri's Prisoner	Sara Craven
The Merciless Travis Wilde	Sandra Marton
A Game with One Winner	Lynn Raye Harris
Heir to a Desert Legacy	Maisey Yates
The Sinful Art of Revenge	Maya Blake
Marriage in Name Only?	Anne Oliver
Waking Up Married	Mira Lyn Kelly
Sparks Fly with the Billionaire	Marion Lennox
A Daddy for Her Sons	Raye Morgan
Along Came Twins…	Rebecca Winters
An Accidental Family	Ami Weaver
A Date with a Bollywood Star	Riya Lakhani
The Proposal Plan	Charlotte Phillips
Their Most Forbidden Fling	Melanie Milburne
The Last Doctor She Should Ever Date	Louisa George

MEDICAL

NYC Angels: Unmasking Dr Serious	Laura Iding
NYC Angels: The Wallflower's Secret	Susan Carlisle
Cinderella of Harley Street	Anne Fraser
You, Me and a Family	Sue MacKay

ROMANCE

A Ring to Secure His Heir	Lynne Graham
What His Money Can't Hide	Maggie Cox
Woman in a Sheikh's World	Sarah Morgan
At Dante's Service	Chantelle Shaw
The English Lord's Secret Son	Margaret Way
The Secret That Changed Everything	Lucy Gordon
The Cattleman's Special Delivery	Barbara Hannay
Her Man in Manhattan	Trish Wylie
At His Majesty's Request	Maisey Yates
Breaking the Greek's Rules	Anne McAllister
The Ruthless Caleb Wilde	Sandra Marton

HISTORICAL

Some Like It Wicked	Carole Mortimer
Born to Scandal	Diane Gaston
Beneath the Major's Scars	Sarah Mallory
Warriors in Winter	Michelle Willingham
A Stranger's Touch	Anne Herries

MEDICAL

A Socialite's Christmas Wish	Lucy Clark
Redeeming Dr Riccardi	Leah Martyn
The Family Who Made Him Whole	Jennifer Taylor
The Doctor Meets Her Match	Annie Claydon
The Doctor's Lost-and-Found Heart	Dianne Drake
The Man Who Wouldn't Marry	Tina Beckett

Mills & Boon® Hardback

May 2013

ROMANCE

A Rich Man's Whim	Lynne Graham
A Price Worth Paying?	Trish Morey
A Touch of Notoriety	Carole Mortimer
The Secret Casella Baby	Cathy Williams
Maid for Montero	Kim Lawrence
Captive in his Castle	Chantelle Shaw
Heir to a Dark Inheritance	Maisey Yates
A Legacy of Secrets	Carol Marinelli
Her Deal with the Devil	Nicola Marsh
One More Sleepless Night	Lucy King
A Father for Her Triplets	Susan Meier
The Matchmaker's Happy Ending	Shirley Jump
Second Chance with the Rebel	Cara Colter
First Comes Baby...	Michelle Douglas
Anything but Vanilla...	Liz Fielding
It was Only a Kiss	Joss Wood
Return of the Rebel Doctor	Joanna Neil
One Baby Step at a Time	Meredith Webber

MEDICAL

NYC Angels: Flirting with Danger	Tina Beckett
NYC Angels: Tempting Nurse Scarlet	Wendy S. Marcus
One Life Changing Moment	Lucy Clark
P.S. You're a Daddy!	Dianne Drake

ROMANCE

Beholden to the Throne	Carol Marinelli
The Petrelli Heir	Kim Lawrence
Her Little White Lie	Maisey Yates
Her Shameful Secret	Susanna Carr
The Incorrigible Playboy	Emma Darcy
No Longer Forbidden?	Dani Collins
The Enigmatic Greek	Catherine George
The Heir's Proposal	Raye Morgan
The Soldier's Sweetheart	Soraya Lane
The Billionaire's Fair Lady	Barbara Wallace
A Bride for the Maverick Millionaire	Marion Lennox

HISTORICAL

Some Like to Shock	Carole Mortimer
Forbidden Jewel of India	Louise Allen
The Caged Countess	Joanna Fulford
Captive of the Border Lord	Blythe Gifford
Behind the Rake's Wicked Wager	Sarah Mallory

MEDICAL

Maybe This Christmas…?	Alison Roberts
A Doctor, A Fling & A Wedding Ring	Fiona McArthur
Dr Chandler's Sleeping Beauty	Melanie Milburne
Her Christmas Eve Diamond	Scarlet Wilson
Newborn Baby For Christmas	Fiona Lowe
The War Hero's Locked-Away Heart	Louisa George